THE QUEEN'S RIVAL

Raymond Wemmlinger

SAPERE
BOOKS

THE QUEEN'S RIVAL

Published by Sapere Books.

24 Trafalgar Road, Ilkley, LS29 8HH

saperebooks.com

ISBN: 978-0-85495-543-5

1

Brougham Castle, 1553

What my father had just told me was beyond belief. "Surely you jest!" I managed to utter.

His expression didn't change. "No," he said, quietly but firmly.

I could only stare incredulously at him. I was Lady Margaret Clifford, cousin to King Edward VI, great-granddaughter to the first Tudor king and seventh in line for the throne of England. As the sole child of Henry Clifford, the Earl of Cumberland, and Lady Eleanor Brandon, I was the greatest territorial heiress in the country. And Father was standing here proposing that I be married to a mere knight!

But Father never jested. In the six years since we had moved permanently to Brougham Castle after my mother had died, he had seldom even smiled. Melancholy wrapped itself around him.

"My lord Father," I finally managed to say, "have you lost your wits?"

We stood nearly eye to eye, but not quite. Although at sixteen I was taller than most women, his height was still greater. My mother had been tall too, with brown hair and hazel eyes, but I had my father's look — lean and angular, with a pale complexion and brown eyes. But my long hair was as thick and voluminous as my mother's had been, and its deep brown had a red tint — the legacy of the red hair of the Tudors. But Father always said my strongest Tudor inheritance was my stubbornness, something I would now put to good use.

I held his gaze. "I will not marry Sir Andrew Dudley," I said. "It is shocking to me that you suggest I even meet with him." I clenched one hand into a fist and angrily slapped it into the palm of the other. "Oh! That you would even invite him here!"

"I didn't invite him. You didn't hear what I said, Margaret. I received a letter from the king saying he had told Sir Andrew to visit to see if you liked each other sufficiently for a possible marriage."

"That boy-king is a fool!" I burst out.

"Be careful what you say," Father replied sharply.

I opened my mouth but decided to heed his warning. I knew he was right. Beneath his mild and scholarly demeanour was the heart of a great northern magnate, an earl descended from a family that had survived the wars of the Plantagenets and used their wits and determination to prosper. It was very fitting that the Clifford family motto was one simple but powerful word: *Henceforth*.

"The king is no longer a boy. He is not much younger than you," Father continued. "In fact, he has never had the luxury of being a boy, what with the responsibilities of his position since his father died."

Remorse pricked at me, and I felt a wave of sympathy for this cousin who I had only met once, many years ago. His father, King Henry VIII, had died a few months before my mother had. And Edward's mother, the late king's third wife Jane Seymour, had died giving birth to him. Edward would have had to grow up very quickly. His life at the centre of the court would have been very different from mine in a quiet, beautiful northern castle.

But there were times, especially lately, when the isolation of life in the castle had grown wearisome, and I had longed for more excitement. Increasingly, marriage had appeared to be the solution, preferably to a powerful noble from an ancient family with great wealth and many homes, including one in London. For the past two years, Father had received letters from every prominent English lord with a marriageable son. Nothing had gone far enough to call for an introduction, and his response to my persistent questions had always been that the time was not yet right. I suspected that he believed the stars and planets were not yet favourably aligned. He studied them himself, unwilling to rely on the advice of astrologers the way others did.

"The king holds enormous power," Father went on. "You must never regard his requests lightly; to even appear to oppose him can be a very dangerous thing. I have seen many destroyed who did not understand this. We must at least appear to consider this inappropriate marriage. With a little skill and cleverness, we will avoid any tie to the family of that upstart Duke of Northumberland, in ways that the parents of your cousin Jane were unable to."

It was little more than a week since my first cousin Lady Jane Grey had married Guildford Dudley, a younger son of the Duke of Northumberland, and a nephew of the Sir Andrew Dudley whom the king was now proposing for me.

A breeze, cool and smelling of spring, touched my face, and I saw the window was open, despite the fire in the hearth. Although it was June, the Cumberland evenings and nights were still cool, and this large room Father used as both his bedroom and study was on the third floor, the highest part of the castle. It was remote, which gave him the solitude he craved for his reading, and high enough up to give him a view of the stars. The open window told me he'd been viewing them before I'd come in. "The movements of the stars do not control our lives," he'd told me long ago. "They incline, but do not dictate. Ultimately, we have our will. But it can help to consult them."

The room was very large, the stone walls uncovered by tapestries. At night the walls appeared to recede into the shadows, beyond the reach of candlelight.

Jane stood ahead of me in the line of succession, as did her mother and Jane's two sisters. Her life had been the opposite of mine: her parents were prominent at court, Reformers in religion as the king was, with strong social and political ties to those whom he favoured, especially John Dudley, the Duke of Northumberland and President of the King's Privy Council. I'd only met the Greys once on a trip to Bradgate, their home in the south, the year before my mother had died. My mother and her older sister hadn't been close, and my parents had been reclusive. That trip to London and then Bradgate had been the only one I could remember that took us away from our homes in the north.

Everyone at Bradgate had been welcoming and pleasant, but what I remembered most was that they had all been so very different from us. Jane, who was the same age as me, had been my exact opposite. In appearance she had been short and fair with light golden-red hair, and very subtle in her movements. She had spoken with little variation in her tone or expression, and her comments were studied. She'd seemed to solemnly consider everything I said as though it had the greatest importance — even a slight remark about the weather — and there had been pauses before she replied to any question or statement, which had always left me feeling as if I had said the wrong thing.

I'd felt awkward and clumsy around her. Sitting beside her when we'd dined had been an ordeal; her manners had been perfect, her delicate hands expertly handling her silver knife and spoon. Never had I dropped so much food on my lap or trailed my sleeves in so many sauces. One time I somehow even ended up with pastry crumbs in my hair, which Jane, with one deft flick of her napkin, had reached over and brushed away before anyone else could see. She had been kind in that way, but when I'd thanked her, she had always replied that it was her Christian duty.

Religion had clearly been more important to Jane than anything else, even more so than her royal heritage. Before we'd journeyed south that year, my parents had explained to me the great divide in England between the followers of the old Catholic ways, and the new Reformers. Laws had changed, starting in the time of King Henry and continuing in the reign of his son. Statues, stained glass and precious plate had been removed from the churches, altar stones had been replaced with wooden communion tables, and the ceremonies had transformed. In the north, there had been much resistance to the changes, but the south had largely embraced the new reforms. My parents had warned me not to mention that we had merely hidden the altar stones, vestments and plate used in many of the chapels of our own castles and manors, and that Mass was still said as it always had been. The rich and beautifully coloured stained-glass windows had also remained.

Even at ten years old Jane had clearly favoured the new religion, and her education had been full of it. She'd been able to quote scripture better than anyone I had ever met, and she was already fluent in both Latin and Greek. Her formidable intellect had already been recognised, and she had sent the king several perfectly composed letters full of Reformist sentiments that he had praised lavishly to the entire court.

In the years after our trip, rumours had reached us in our castle at Brougham that the king would marry Jane, she being his perfect match in intellect, station and belief. Therefore, I'd been shocked to learn that she was to be wed to Guildford Dudley, the rather unexceptional third son of the duke.

It had been the servants who'd told me of the wedding, and at first, I'd been sure they were wrong. But when I'd confronted Father about it, he'd confirmed it was true. "Northumberland is much favoured by the king. He shares his religious beliefs. His power grows stronger all the time."

Jane's younger sister Catherine was to be married at the same time, although it would not be consummated until she was older, and Mary, the youngest, had been betrothed. The girls had been matched with sons of two of the most important noblemen in the kingdom, both Reformers and allies of Northumberland. And the duke's daughter Catherine Dudley had been married to another, a distant cousin of mine with his own claim to the throne.

It was clear Northumberland was being empowered by the king through the marriages, as was Jane's branch of the royal family. I'd desperately wanted to attend the double wedding in London. As the first cousin of the two brides, I'd be one of the most honoured guests, and as an eligible bride myself I would no doubt be courted. It was the perfect avenue for escape from my dull life in the north. It mattered little that Jane was marrying a social upstart beneath her, and that many of the guests would snicker behind their hands. For me, it could be a superb setting for my introduction as a person of importance in England.

Father had flatly refused. "There is more to these marriages than meets the eye," he had said darkly. "And there are rumours that the king is ill. The Lady Mary is next in the line of succession, and she is of the old religion. Much would change for the Reformers, should she come to the throne. No, we will stay as far away from these marriages as we can."

His aversion to such matches could not have been clearer. But now, he was telling me to consider marriage to a man with strong ties to the very core of this Reformist faction.

"Who is this Sir Andrew Dudley?" I asked suspiciously. "You said he is Guildford's uncle?"

"The duke's younger brother."

"He must be your age," I said disparagingly.

"We are of the same generation. I may have met him years ago, but I don't remember. Northumberland in his younger days was in the circle surrounding your grandfather, the Duke of Suffolk, and we occasionally crossed paths. I may have met Sir Andrew. I might remember when I see him." He gestured to a letter on the table beside him. "The king writes that he served with distinction against the Scots on both land and sea, as captain. He was also captain at Guisnes."

"A soldier," I said with disgust. "He probably smells." I wrinkled my nose.

"For nearly all of Edward's reign he has been one of his four chief gentlemen. He is Keeper of the Royal Household at Westminster and Keeper of Jewels and Robes. Earlier this year he was also entrusted with a diplomatic mission to the emperor. I doubt he smells."

"How many times has he been married? And how long has he been a widower?"

Father hesitated, implying that I wouldn't like the answer. Would it be six times, like old King Henry? Eventually, he said, "The king writes that he has never married."

That was even worse. It was very unusual for a man in his forties not to have ever married. "He must be repulsive!"

"Well, clearly the king favours him. The king's gentlemen come closer to him than all others, and have his ear and confidence." Father shook his head. "No, Margaret, I doubt there will be anything personally objectionable beyond his lowly status. It is not the man himself we must be most careful of. There is something much larger that we must not let ourselves be drawn into."

The candles on the table flickered in the breeze from the window. "What do the stars predict?" I asked.

"Nothing of clarity. The most I can venture to say is a time of confusion and uncertainty."

"I mean for me."

"A time of change."

A time of change. The words rang ominously in my head. What else could that mean but marriage? "I will not marry Sir Andrew!" I said as I stamped my foot on the floor.

"This visit is only to see if you like each other, which is common practice. You have only to meet him and be cordial during the time he is here. Afterward, I will write to the king to say he is not to your liking, which will be believable, given the vast age difference. This is the best course I can take. It's much better than objecting to his low status as a knight." Father paused. "Had I done that, the king would simply have arranged to elevate him to the rank of lord or baron. But an objection based on age or personal distaste is not so easily overcome."

Grudgingly, I acknowledged the wisdom of the plan. It would be the easiest way of ridding ourselves of him, without offending the king. "When do you want this visit to take place?" I asked reluctantly.

"He arrives tomorrow morning. Early, not long after dawn."

Astonishment and resentment soared in me. Father had waited until the last possible moment to tell me, ensuring I had no chance to escape to one of our hunting lodges or nearby manors. "I will not marry him!" I shouted.

I seized the king's letter from the table, ran to the fireplace and thrust it into the flames. Turning back to Father, I saw he was standing still, his gaze fixed on the disappearing letter. This was not the reaction I had hoped to provoke in him.

On the table, beside where the letter had been, was an open astrology book, the visible pages full of strange diagrams and calculations. I ran over and snatched it up, intending for it to share the letter's fate.

This time, Father's protest was immediate. "No!" he cried, stepping forward with an outstretched hand.

I stopped, realising that I was about to deprive him of one of his few pleasures in life. It was love that made me stop, and instead throw the book on the floor, where it landed with a thud.

Father exhaled sharply, his shoulders sagging with relief. "That book is irreplaceable," he murmured. "It was years before my Italian agent could find me a copy."

"My grandmother was a queen of France!" I shouted in response, but with no sense of where the words had come from. But my next statement was deliberate. "My mother would never have agreed to this."

Father's face closed instantly. I had hurt him, as I'd wanted to. The heavy cloak of melancholy surrounded him and he nearly disappeared within it, retreating to wherever he went to survive his lingering grief.

Suddenly shocked that I could have been so cruel, I turned and ran from the room, past his waiting servants in the narrow passage outside the door, and started down the spiral staircase.

"Touch the wall," the servant immediately behind me with a taper warned. But I'd taken the stairs so many times that I was confident I wouldn't misstep.

2

In the morning, Mrs Brograve drew back the curtains of my bed at first light, just as she always had for as long as I could remember. As usual, my other gentlewomen were at the foot of the bed, smiling down at me.

"Good morning, little swan," Mrs Brograve said cheerfully, and the three women echoed in unison, "Good morning, little swan."

It was the ritual we repeated every morning. The women's cheerfulness was forced, but Mrs Brograve's was genuine. She was always good-natured in a no-nonsense way. Middle-aged, short and squat, she supervised my care and attendance with domestic expertise and a force of will that dominated everyone in the castle. My other gentlewomen were terrified of her, and followed her orders precisely. She'd established the enthusiastic morning greeting years ago, right after my mother had died and she'd stepped forward as a partial surrogate. No doubt she'd felt a bereaved child required cheering, and she'd been right. I'd been fond of the greeting for years, but lately it had begun to strike me as ridiculous. The women were now becoming elderly, and on some days their wide-eyed expressions and stretched smiles looked like bizarre grimaces.

This morning, the greeting was particularly grating, especially since I'd been awake for some time, brooding over the imminent arrival of Sir Andrew Dudley, and devising a plan to dispose of the matter my own way. By the time the curtains were drawn back, I had resolved that this morning, the little swan was not going to be getting out of bed.

"I'm ill," I announced. "I won't be getting up today."

At the foot of the bed the women stared blankly at me, uncertain what to do next. All three blinked, then simultaneously turned their heads to Mrs Brograve. There was a short silence as she calculated her response. Then she plunged into her morning routine, reaching beside the pillows for the basket with the jug of weak wine and loaf of bread I was always given in case I grew hungry during the night.

She opened the basket and picked up the loaf, running her fingers over the end I had eaten from, and then she shook the jug to determine whether I had drunk from it. She gestured towards me with the loaf and said pointedly, "The little swan was well enough to gobble up some breadcrumbs."

Indeed I had, for nourishment while devising my plan. But I ignored her and pulled the covers all the way up. "Tell my father I'm staying in bed."

The women stared, full of gleeful anticipation of the scene about to unfold. They'd witnessed many between us and were well aware that Mrs Brograve was the only person in the castle who was a match for my will.

"Now, now," she cooed, but with an iron undertone, "you fly right up and you'll see how much better you feel once you're on your feet!" She gently but firmly started to pull the blanket away, but my fists tightened and held it in place.

"No," I said. "I'm ill. I'm remaining here today. And maybe for a few days until I'm completely better."

"You need to get up." Her tone was suddenly sharp. "You know very well why."

I ignored her. The image of a possible Sir Andrew Dudley, with a middle-aged paunch, vanishing hair, missing teeth and at least one ugly battle scar on his face flickered before my eyes. My grip on the blanket tightened. No one ever married for love, but a comely appearance mattered. Marriage, especially for the nobility, was about advantageous alliances between families of status, with the ultimate goal of producing children. And if two people couldn't stand physical intimacy with each other, how successful would that be?

Father's plan to avoid the marriage was sound, in that the king would have no counterargument to our not finding each other appealing. Certainly, I wouldn't find Sir Andrew so. But what Father was not taking into account was the likelihood of Sir Andrew finding me quite suitable for marriage in that regard. Although I knew I wasn't a beauty — I'd overheard enough whispered remarks from the female servants — I wasn't bad to look at, with looks sufficient not to repel any suitor. Sir Andrew would probably find me satisfactory in a way that I would not reciprocate, and, given his closeness to the king, he just might be able to use his influence to force the marriage. No, Father's plan was flawed indeed. Better for Sir Andrew not to even lay eyes on me.

"I'm ill," I insisted. "Very ill. I doubt I'll be out of bed all week."

Mrs Brograve took a step backward, but her shoulders squared as she planted both hands on her hips. She was readying herself for battle. "Lady Margaret," she began. "I believe —"

She was interrupted by a low rumbling and rattling of chains; two floors directly below us, the front gate of the castle was being lifted. Usually everyone came and went by the smaller postern gate, but the large main one was raised to welcome visitors of distinction. The guards had sighted Sir Andrew Dudley arriving in the distance.

Mrs Brograve and all three women's heads immediately swivelled to look through the two windows overlooking the gate. The light of the newly risen sun was pouring into my room, announcing the day would be fine. But fine day or not, I wasn't getting up. I pulled the blanket up over my head. "I'm ill!" I nearly screamed through the fabric. "Ill, ill, ill!"

There was a scurrying of feet, telling me the others had rushed to the window. I waited tensely. Then, one of them said with awe, "So many horses!"

"At least ten," breathed another. "And how smart they look!"

"And look at all those bundles piled high on the ones in the rear."

I lifted my head out from under the blanket. Two women were peering through one window, and the third was with Mrs Brograve at the other. Outside, the sound of the horses' hooves drew closer.

"Gifts," said Mrs Brograve decisively. "They're gifts, they are. All loaded onto those poor beasts. Imagine, all the way from London like that. Well, he wouldn't dare come here with anything less. It is the home of a grand earl, isn't it?"

I propped myself up on my elbows. *Gifts. Gifts from London.*

"The man out in front must be the one in charge," someone said. "The one in the fur-trimmed cloak."

"He rides well."

"Must be a fine gentleman."

A fine gentleman? I sat up.

"But he hasn't got a hat on," Mrs Brograve said disapprovingly. "What kind of a gentleman goes visiting without a hat?"

"But look, the man behind him is carrying it for him, tucked under his arm. The gentleman just seems to be enjoying the morning air and light."

The sound of the horses' hooves was louder now, as were the voices of the riders.

"Well, what does he look like?" I called sullenly. "The man in front?"

They were so enthralled they didn't even hear me. One of the women said excitedly, "With so many attendants, he must be here on official business!"

"I heard yesterday that we are all to dine in the Great Hall today," Mrs Brograve replied knowingly.

"What does he look like?" I shouted. It was maddening to be ignored by one's own attendants.

Finally, Mrs Brograve and one of the others turned to me with vaguely startled expressions. "Oh, little swan," Mrs Brograve said vaguely. "What did you ask?"

The shouts and laughter outside were strong; they were almost at the gate. In an instant it would be too late. I threw off the covers and dashed to the window, the two women barely able to get out of my way. Looking out, I was just able to see a tall man with straight and graceful carriage ride his horse into the castle. It had been a quick glimpse, not enough for a lasting impression. But I had managed to see a head of silver hair, stirring slightly in the breeze, and I had heard the tone of command in his voice as he'd called out a greeting to the guards.

I watched as the line of other riders followed him, at the end of which came the servants leading the horses laden with gifts. The size and number of those neatly wrapped bundles was impressive, and my eyes lingered on them as the horses trotted past the gate.

My longing to escape my quiet life rose within me, but I pushed it down. No matter how many gifts he brought, it was important to remember that Sir Andrew Dudley was a mere knight.

I took a step back toward the bed, intent on returning to it. But Mrs Brograve had seized the opportunity to pull the cover tight and was now straightening the pillows. It would be a battle to get past her to return to it.

"So many gifts," one of the women whispered. "And all brought from London."

Though I wouldn't be able to keep the gifts after I rejected Sir Andrew's suit, I couldn't help sharing the woman's excitement. Most of our luxuries came from no farther away than York — an important city, but London was the capital. I'd only been there once, when I was ten years old, but the magnificent palaces had left a lasting impression on me, as had the crowds, banquets, plays, games and music.

I watched the woman at the window as she continued to look out, her pale blue eyes shining. She was of the local gentry, a knight's younger daughter who had never married and instead spent her life as an attendant to the Clifford family women, first my aunts and then me. When I was younger, she had seemed ageless, as had the others, but recently the passage of time had taken a noticeable toll on her and her companions, who were all of similar years. Delicate lines had appeared around her eyes, nose and mouth, her hair had lost its colour, and a quietness had come over her as she'd faded with age. There had been a certain beauty to it, but I'd never thought to question whether she was happy. Watching her now, so in awe of guests of no particular distinction, I realised that life had passed her by.

It could have been worse for her, I justified. Positions in the household of an earl were not easily found and held status. But I wondered whether she and the other two women were disappointed that they had never married or had children.

Noblewomen were usually married at seventeen, sometimes earlier, without consummation. But my cousin the Lady Mary, King Edward's eldest sister, was still unmarried at thirty-seven. The Lady Elizabeth, his other sister, was nearly twenty. Their father had been unable to decide on suitable husbands for them in his lifetime, and in his will he had left authority over the choice to the Privy Council.

For the first time it occurred to me that there were those who might not want a woman with a claim to the throne to marry at all, or produce a male child. At thirty-seven, Mary was already drawing close to the time when she would no longer be able to. And I had little doubt that age was already beginning to alter her in the same way it had altered my women.

Perhaps it wasn't so unfortunate that my cousin Jane had married a man of lower station. Perhaps she was fortunate to be married at all.

Mrs Brograve was finishing the bed. Without looking at me, she said, "You need to hurry to be on time for prayers."

"Since I'm up, I may as well stay up," I said grandly. "I'll wear my green velvet dress. The new one, from York. And one of the English hoods." The English-style hoods, with their wide angles, suited me better than the curving French ones.

I seldom dressed so well merely for morning prayers in the chapel, but it would be imperative for Sir Andrew to understand the kind of life we were used to in the castle, that Cumberland was not a place where we all lived in poverty. He would need to be impressed that I was likely the wealthiest woman in England, and had a claim to the throne. The green of my dress, the Tudor colour, would help make that clear. No matter how fine his gifts, he could never be a suitable husband for me. But it would still be nice to see what he'd brought.

He wasn't at prayers. Neither was Father, which was unusual, since he was diligent about setting an example for the household, even though he disliked the saying of prayers in English and the other Reformist changes. But today it was clear he was with the newly arrived guest in the offices beside the barracks; as I crossed the courtyard on my return from the chapel, my women holding my dress so the hem wouldn't trail in the dirt, there were several members of Sir Andrew's retinue out front of it, lounging in the morning sun. They stood and bowed as I passed, their stares telling me they well knew the reason for their journey to Brougham Castle.

"None of them were at prayers," one of my women murmured disapprovingly. All three of them liked the religious changes of the past decade. Unlike me, they did not understand Latin, although they had been educated. The translation into English of the prayers and services had therefore benefitted them, as had the availability of the Bible in English back in the reign of King Henry. But in the north of England they were the exception. Most people, gentry and common folk alike, preferred the mystery and awe of the old Latin Mass and prayers.

King Edward had shown a passion for religious reform, and from the beginning of his reign the changes instigated by his father had progressed. The latest, including a new Book of Common Prayer, had been only a year ago. My women had been enthusiastic, but there'd been grumbling among others at Brougham, including Mrs Brograve. And Father had said grimly, "There'll be trouble over this. The changes go too far. It will be hard for anyone to see the old Mass in these new services." But for me it was all still close enough to the old way of worshipping. The changes didn't seem particularly important, and discussions about them bored me. I privately doubted that God cared whether prayers were in English or Latin so long as people remembered to say them.

But the king felt otherwise and was the leader of the Reformers, who surrounded him at court. My cousin Jane and her parents were members of that group, as was the Duke of Northumberland. Sir Andrew, being the duke's brother and close to the king, would of course be a Reformer as well, and I'd fully expected him to be at morning prayers. His absence didn't trouble me, but I couldn't help but wonder if he would have missed them if still in London, under the watchful eye of the king.

The most stately rooms in the castle were on the floor below mine, and they were where Sir Andrew would be lodged. My women hesitated reluctantly when I shooed them upstairs ahead of me, saying I wished to see that the arrangements were comfortable. They even began to protest; not only were they supposed to remain with me, but they wanted to see the gifts. But one quick, sharp "Go!" sent them on their way. There would be time for them to see the gifts later, and without them I could be in and out quickly before Sir Andrew returned.

I knew Mrs Brograve would soon come to search for me, so I hurried across the large centre room and into the one behind. I'd guessed correctly: one of Sir Andrew's attendants was deftly unwrapping the gifts and setting them out on the table.

The man, small and wiry, was the one who had ridden behind Sir Andrew, holding his hat. Seeing me, he stopped, clearly wondering how to respond. "My lady," he said after a moment, bowing. He then continued his work.

In his hands, a silver and gilt pitcher emerged from the wrapping. It glittered beckoningly as he placed it on the table, drawing me to it, and I went and picked it up. It was encrusted with pearls, jacinths and rubies, so lovely that my breath hitched. My gaze travelled over the other captivating riches already unwrapped and spread out. There was a large leaf-shaped gold brooch, set with emeralds and pearls. Next to it was a gold chain belt, enamelled with black and sprinkled with agates, and beside that was a gold coronet, set with rubies, pearls and diamonds. Four or five gold rings set with diamonds sparkled in a little pile beside them.

I longed to touch these exquisite jewels, but I clutched my hands together, trying to contain my astonishment.

There was more. My eyes ran over white silk gloves, brocaded purses, an exquisitely carved chess set, cloth of silver and gold, and blue and gold embroidered hangings and covers.

The attendant was unwrapping the final gift, and I watched, fascinated, as a strange metal disc was revealed. Seeing my interest, he offered it to me.

I took it carefully. It was about the size of my hand and made of gilded brass, with movable parts, full of numbers and markings. Some were the zodiac signs; it was clearly an instrument to calculate the positions of the stars.

"The astrolabe is for your father," said a male voice behind me.

I whirled around to see Sir Andrew standing halfway between me and the door, his arms folded, his manner suggesting he had been there for some time, watching me. I stared, taking him in. Anyone would regard him as handsome, even though he was clearly middle-aged. He was tall and solidly built, but trim, without the paunch I'd seen in other men his age. His hair was still abundant, with streaks of its original colour showing between the silver, and his neatly trimmed beard was still entirely dark. His face was oval with well-balanced features, his complexion smooth and tan. His eyes were a dazzling shade of blue, the liveliness of which became even more apparent as he strode toward me.

"Lady Margaret," he said, bowing, "you must forgive my rough attire. I hadn't expected to meet you so early in the day."

He was still wearing his travelling clothes: a slashed brown leather jerkin over a dark red doublet and hose, with tall leather boots and a black sword belt and hanger on the side of his waist.

He gently took the astrolabe from my hands. "Lord Cumberland told me you would be at your studies now, and I would meet you at dinner." His voice was low and even, and he had a London accent. This was no gruff soldier, but a perfect courtier. "The astrolabe is ancient, from Greece. They are rare. Before becoming mine, this one was the property of Baron Sudeley."

His eyelids fluttered; no doubt he was remembering the unfortunate fate of Baron Sudeley, Thomas Seymour, the younger of the king's two maternal uncles. Both were now dead, executed as traitors.

"A foolish man," he added quickly, with delicate but unmistakable disdain. "But it isn't easy to be the younger brother of a great duke, no matter how favoured by the king." He ran his finger over the astrolabe and looked down at it, frowning. "The astrolabe is a valuable tool for navigation at sea, and surely Baron Sudeley would have used it so. But it is often used to seek the guidance and direction of the stars for the affairs of men." He glanced up at me, as if seeking my opinion. He spoke as though we were old friends. "I wonder if Baron Sudeley used it for that. If so, his results were poor, considering how tragically he misjudged certain ... situations."

He stepped back, with one hand holding the instrument up and away from him. "I have captained many ships, and have used an astrolabe to navigate, with good effect. But I use nothing to predict my future. I create my own."

His blue eyes fixed upon my face. His eyelids fluttered, and I knew he found me pleasing, but it wouldn't have mattered if he did not. He had already decided I was the future he would be creating for himself.

His audacity was startling but admirable. As I struggled to find a reply, he placed the astrolabe on the table. Then he leaned forward, his fingers lightly touching the jewelled coronet. He turned his blue eyes back to me and smiled.

Confusion, apprehension and excitement tore through me. Never had I been so unsure of myself. It felt important that I reply, but no words would form on my lips. Instead, I turned and rushed out of the room, certain that he was watching.

3

Later that morning, just before dinner, we were formally introduced. Sir Andrew was dressed differently, in a jerkin of cloth of silver, a black doublet and hose, and a sumptuous wide-shouldered grey box coat, trimmed with sable. Neither of us saw fit to mention we had already met, and I wondered if the charade amused him as much as it did me. I'd quickly recovered my composure after my retreat from his rooms. At first, I had been angry with myself, but then I decided it mattered little if I had not impressed him. I didn't want to. And I had certainly read too much into his touching the coronet. Many others stood before me in the succession, and he knew it. Besides, I would never allow myself to be a stepping stone for the ambition of a mere knight, no matter how poised and well-mannered he was.

But there was no denying his gifts were impressive. I felt glad I had seen them before as he now presented them again, surrounded by my gentlewomen, Mrs Brograve and Father's gentlemen. I was able to remain aloof while my women gasped with admiration, and Mrs Brograve said softly, "Gifts fit for a queen." Even Father received the astrolabe with a rare glint of interest in his eyes. Sir Andrew might well have known the reason for my composure and restraint, but what he thought was inconsequential. I counted it in his favour that he did not try to alter the impression I was making on the others. I even lightly rested my hand on his arm when he offered it as we went in to dinner.

We seldom ate in the Great Hall with the rest of the hundred or so members of the household; we only did so when we had visitors of importance. Mrs Brograve had told me that since dawn, efforts had been made to not only see that the meal was sumptuous, but that it was served properly. But the servants' unfamiliarity with correct procedures showed from the start. We arrived on the dais to overlook a scene of chaos as the ushers futilely attempted to arrange everyone at table according to rank, since the household usually ignored protocol and sat where they wanted, even when Father and I ate with them. Sir Andrew's attendants stood to one side, snickering.

Sir Andrew sat on one side of Father on the dais, I in my usual place on the other, close enough to be able to hear Sir Andrew's remarks. The disasters continued during the meal. The fashionable sound of trumpets announcing the arrival of each new course, which we'd never done before, provoked laughter and jeers instead of gratitude for the food. The respectful donning of caps by the servants at the sound of the trumpets was a fiasco, and so disruptive that it was abandoned after one or two courses. On the opposite dais, the musicians were trying new songs for the first time, and sounded terrible. Some dishes, the ones favoured by Father and often prepared, were fine, but the new ones were awful. I was particularly revolted by the swan, which we'd never had before. It seemed a bad omen, a snide joke on the part of one of the chefs, since everyone in the castle knew of Mrs Brograve's name for me. At another time I might have run into the kitchen, found out who had done it and had them beaten, but today I couldn't, because of our guest. Instead I gripped my spoon, smiled politely and chose the stewed pheasant instead. On the other side of Father, Sir Andrew requested the swan. But I wondered if he'd try it after all, since right then a voice in the hall proclaimed, "Ugh! The swan is too tough!"

By the time it was over and we'd been presented with bowls to wash our fingers, one of which the servant spilled on the table, I was certain Sir Andrew had been convinced we were uncouth bumpkins, and he would be all too willing to tell everyone in London of the debacle in revenge when his suit was rejected. Appropriate suitors would hear of it and stay away, regardless of my wealth and position. I would end up married to some minor viscount or baron and be sent to a damp castle for the rest of my life, ignored by everyone.

But if Sir Andrew had been offended or disdainful of anything, it didn't show; he thanked Father for the sumptuous banquet, sounding sincere. Again, he offered his arm as we returned to the main part of the castle.

"Lady Margaret," he said as I placed my hand on his sleeve, "you were missed at the wedding of our relatives last month." Unnecessarily, and a little remotely as though his thoughts had returned to that event, he clarified, "My nephew Guildford and your cousin Jane." Then, much more pointedly, he added, "I, in particular, was disappointed when I learned the earl had refused the invitation. I had so hoped to meet you there."

"My father has not returned to London since the death of my mother, Lady Eleanor. He cannot abide some of the places where they lived together during happier times. For the past six years we have visited neither our other home in Skipton, nor London."

"Both have been diminished by your absence."

It was flattery, but the plain and direct way he said it made it sound sincere. "How could I press my father to overcome his grief for my own pursuit of pleasure?" I demurely turned my face away. He would never know how I had begged to go to the wedding.

"It was to the brides' advantage," he said simply. "You would have eclipsed them."

"The wedding was splendid, no doubt."

"Oh, yes. Everyone said it was the most lavish one they could remember. Many, many people attended. Fortunately, my brother's home is quite large, with expansive grounds. Even outside it seemed that all of London was trying to catch a glimpse of the brides; the Strand at the rear of the house was thronged, and some even found their way to the waterway steps on the Thames. I fear many were disappointed, since the wedding was performed right there in the chapel at Durham House."

"Was Jane very lovely?"

"She was — to the detriment of her sister, I must admit. With Jane's carriage and stately manner, she was the most impressive young woman there. There was a group of them, you see, sixteen in total — one for each year of Jane's age. They were all dressed in white, with bride lace and rosemary on their sleeves. Jane alone wore cloth of gold, with a cloth of silver mantle."

"I find your memory impressive, Sir Andrew."

"I am Keeper of Jewels and Robes. It has taught me to notice fine things. And the jewels and garments were gifts from the king, which I helped select from the wardrobe. Lady Jane's headpiece of green velvet, surrounded by jewels, was my special recommendation."

"Green," I remarked. "Of course, green."

"The Tudor colour. Beneath it, Jane's red-gold hair, beautifully combed, hung down her back. She looked like a queen."

There was a pause. I couldn't tell whether it was intentional or not, and it brought to mind his earlier touching of the coronet. I shifted my hand on his arm before it could tremble. "Tell me more of the wedding," I said.

"What more is there to say?" He gestured dismissively with his free hand. "All the rooms in Durham House were hung with crimson and gold tissue, and the guests were resplendent in their colourful finery. Then there was a masque, led by Guildford and Jane, with all the young people participating. And then feasting, for hours and hours. I fear all the livestock surrounding London was depleted by the event."

"Did the king dance gracefully?"

Again, there was a brief silence before he answered. "The king was not present. He was ill."

His simple answer spoke volumes. The king's presence at the wedding would have been expected, given the importance of the brides and grooms. If he had not attended, he was very ill indeed.

Something important was happening in London, something surrounding the throne, and I was being left out of it. It involved my birthright, the line of succession, which should have placed me at the forefront of English society. I should have been at the wedding, with all those guests dancing in the crimson- and gold-draped rooms of Durham House. I should have played a prominent role in the masque. The crowds at the gates should have struggled to see me as well.

Sir Andrew's wrist beneath my hand suddenly felt very strong. His earlier remark about having hoped to meet me at the wedding had not been lost upon me. Had I been present, there was no question that he would have seen me in my rightful place. Afterwards, when people spoke of the magnificence of the wedding, and the loveliness of the brides, they would also have remembered that Lady Margaret Clifford had made an impression there too. Instead, I'd been stuck away at Brougham Castle, as I had been for many years, and might very well be for years to come.

Resentment surged through me; Father had no right to deprive me of my rightful place. Of course, he was trying to protect me, but for the first time I saw the extent to which his thoughts were clouded by grief. Perhaps it was time for me to take matters into my own hands regarding my future.

Beneath my hand, the fabric of Sir Andrew's sleeve was soft and smooth, and pleasant to the touch. "Did the king's sisters dance well?" I asked.

He stopped and turned slightly towards me so that I too had to stop walking and look at him. From the corner of my eye I could see Father trailing behind us in the corridor, talking to his gentlemen.

Sir Andrew's blue eyes scrutinised my face; he was trying to ascertain how much I understood. "Neither the Lady Mary nor the Lady Elizabeth were able to attend," he said eventually.

I waited for him to add an explanation, such as their living too far from London, but he did not. He was making no attempt to dissuade me from what he already thought I knew: there had been politics involved in the wedding.

Father came up beside us. "The day is fine," he said. "Shall we hunt?"

"I'd wanted to bring you a falcon, Lord Cumberland," Sir Andrew said. "But the only peregrine of suitable quality escaped as we prepared to leave. It didn't return. All the falconers said they could never remember when another had done the same."

Father carried his favourite peregrine, followed by the three falconers who attended the mews at Brougham, each with a bird perched on his wrist. "None of your own, my lady?" Sir

Andrew asked as we rode out into the fields, where there would be abundant prey.

Before I could answer, Father replied, "Lady Margaret has not yet the patience for training one."

The comment irritated me, and I rode apart from them. Usually the soar of a falcon gave me feelings of exhilaration and giddy freedom, but today it did not. Sullenly, I wished I had trained one of my own to now have perched upon my wrist, ready to fly off and bring back the largest prize of all.

"This will be our last today," Father said as his bird took flight. "The hour is late, and supper will be waiting for us." Behind him, a servant held the three hares already caught.

The peregrine soared until it was nearly out of sight, and then began its dive toward the earth, its target invisible to us. "It will be another hare," Father said knowingly. "Sufficient as our final catch."

When it landed, Father galloped off himself to retrieve it and the hapless hare. I was seized with a desire to escape, to return to the castle where I was not consigned to the role of spectator. Unnoticed, I turned my horse and began trotting away.

I'd gone some distance before I heard another rider approaching, and Sir Andrew appeared beside me. Pointedly I tugged the reins and went faster, almost galloping. He hadn't expected it, and I surged ahead of him. I would not be so easily caught.

He caught up with me again, and one of his hands swooped over and grabbed the reins of my horse, stopping it.

"You could have fallen," he said reproachfully, though he looked amused.

It was difficult to control a horse when riding side-saddle, but I had more ability with horses then most women. "I prefer speed. As my lord Father said before, I have no patience for slowness."

"You didn't enjoy the hunt?"

"I felt excluded. I wished I had my own falcon."

"I will bring you an eagle."

"They are especially difficult to train for the hunt. Remember, I lack patience."

He pulled the reins of my horse, drawing himself closer. The spring air had invigorated him, as it had me. He seemed much younger than his age and full of life. I'd already noticed how well he rode, with agility and elegance.

He peered at my face, his eyes locking with my own. "I will train it for you," he said, "as I will train others to respect you. Never will you feel excluded again."

Boldly, I returned his stare. "You wish to marry me," I said bluntly.

"Yes," he replied, with equal bluntness.

"Your brother the duke wants it also."

"And the king. He very much wants this marriage."

"But you don't always do as the king wishes. Today, you weren't at prayers. The king wouldn't approve."

At first, he said nothing, gazing off into the distance. He relaxed his hold on the reins somewhat, and our horses moved apart. Finally, he said, "The king cares greatly for religion. I do not. The old ways and the new ways are all the same to me. Sometimes I believe one way, sometimes the other. Sometimes I believe all of it and sometimes none of it. Most days, I don't even think about it." He smiled. "But when I go into battle, I believe all of it, and that God wants me to win. You have to, when you go into battle. Or when you want something. You must really believe God wants you to have it."

"Do you believe God wants you to have me as your wife?"

"Yes. The king believes it even more." He leaned toward me. "But even more than God or the king, I want it. Especially after meeting you here today."

I looked away from him, into the distance, where the sandy stones of the castle were shining pink in the afternoon light. The beauty of it struck me, as it often did. As if he could read my thoughts, Sir Andrew said, "A beautiful home, Brougham Castle. Different, I imagine, in each season. It must be lovely with snow all around it."

He obviously appreciated beauty, whether natural or in life's luxuries. Marriage to such a man would not be uncomfortable.

He went on, "But I would take you away from it. I'm soon to be made Lieutenant Governor of the North, and I need a convenient residence. Skipton Castle would suit. We could live there, in the new wing. Lord Cumberland could reside in the older part of the castle, should he wish."

My grandfather, the first Earl of Cumberland, had added a modern wing to his castle at Skipton in honour of his son's marriage with the king's niece, and as a suitable home for her. The rooms were luxurious and spacious, and separated from the rest of the castle by a fashionable long gallery. Living there would certainly draw attention to our power.

"Lieutenant Governor of the North?" I repeated.

"The king desires it. I will have authority over the whole of the north, and shortly afterward I should be elevated to the peerage. Lady Margaret, you would not long suffer the indignity of marriage to a mere knight."

I could easily see myself at the centre of what would be no less than a royal court of the north. Suddenly I laughed with excitement. "What else does the king desire?"

His answer was quick. "A male Tudor to succeed him. But he has been ill, and recognises that he may not live long enough to produce a son. It troubles him that there are only women as possible successors. For now."

It was a great secret to share; he had already decided he could trust me. The pieces of a great puzzle seemed to slide into place. "And that," I said, "accounts for the urgency of the recent marriages. But what of the Ladies Mary and Elizabeth?"

This time, he hesitated, his eyes narrowing. He was considering how much he should say. "The Lady Mary's religion troubles the king greatly," he confided. "No doubt she would wish to raise any child in the old ways, should she still be capable of bearing one. He is also troubled by her questionable legitimacy, and that of Elizabeth."

Behind us, I could hear the others approaching. "Did you speak of this to my father?" I asked.

"I've spoken of it to no one. Very few know the king's mind regarding this matter — only my brother, my Lord of Suffolk, and one or two others. I tell you in great confidence: earlier, I saw I could trust you. And I have other thoughts that I have shared with no one, not even with my brother. It has come to my attention that the Lady Mary and the Lady Elizabeth are not the only ones whose legitimacy might be of concern. My Lord of Suffolk was precontracted before his marriage to your Aunt Frances. There are many who view such contracts as binding. Presented so, the king might also question the legitimacy of Lady Jane and her two sisters, which would leave only their mother ahead of you in the succession. And she has not conceived a child in more than seven years."

The implications of this were so staggering that I was left unable to speak.

Sir Andrew smiled calmly. "And remember, the king favours me. He desires this marriage as much as my brother does."

In a younger man, his attitude might have appeared foolishly overreaching, but he was of an age that had the benefit of experienced accomplishment. What he wanted just might be within his grasp. His ambition was stunning and gave rise to a vitality that I'd seen in no other man. It attracted me powerfully; I had little doubt that with such a man I could produce many of the male Tudors the king desired.

Father and the rest of the hunting party had almost joined us. Impulsively, I asked, "Why have you never married?"

A veil seemed to draw across his face, and he lowered his eyes. "No woman was ever worth it," he said, unable to conceal the bitterness in his voice. But then he smiled, and once again turned his blue eyes on me. "Until now."

I had no idea if supper was as disastrous as dinner had been, for my whirling thoughts were far removed from the Great Hall. Besides, it no longer mattered: the servants could have dropped every platter, the cooks spoiled every dish, the musicians scraped their instruments discordantly or the entire household stood on the tables and howled like dogs. Such things were now trivialities when viewed against Sir Andrew's plans, which were on the verge of becoming my plans too. My future would be mostly at Skipton Castle. Images of a thriving demi-court there danced through my head: there would be visits from all the nobility and wealthy new merchants, including foreigners. We would make important trips not only to nearby York, but also to London, where we would arrive with a great retinue. Crowds would line the streets as we rode into the city, just like I remembered from our last visit there, years ago.

Once or twice during supper, Father addressed minor remarks to me, and I emerged from my reverie to find him eyeing me with trepidation. He was clearly unhappy that Sir Andrew and I had spent so long in unsupervised conversation at the end of the hunt. At supper he sat between us heavily. Afterward, in the hour preceding our retiring at nine, I presented only one dance, a formal, practised ritual we typically used for the entertainment of our rare guests, before Father called for a display of my music. He wanted no opportunity for Sir Andrew and me to dance together. In the flickering torchlight, I plucked the strings of a harp and then a lute, while my women sang. It did not trouble me that I played so badly that the singing women became confused, and from the side Mrs Brograve stared harshly at me. Once I was established at Skipton, I would have card-playing and games in the evenings after supper. I'd have an entire circle of waiting women around me; I'd keep the older ones, and Mrs Brograve, but I'd add younger ones, who would dance and sing with enthusiasm. And I would never, ever have to touch needlework again.

When we arrived back in my rooms for the night, Sir Andrew's gifts had been delivered there, spread out on a table in the anteroom. In the candlelight, the gold, silver and gems gleamed even more alluringly than they had in daylight, and my women rushed over to them. But Mrs Brograve shooed them away, and had the servants gather the gifts and lock them up. "The earl told me to make sure they are safe," she said. "He wants nothing missing when they're sent back to London." She chuckled. "Imagine a knight thinking he could marry our little swan."

I turned away and said nothing. Soon, very soon, she would see the little swan was fully grown and had wide enough wings to fly away.

In the morning, I had barely dressed when I heard the clanging and rattling of the front gate being drawn. I'd known Sir Andrew was to leave, but not that early. Ruthlessly brushing aside my protesting women and nearly pushing Mrs Brograve out of the way, I rushed downstairs to the courtyard.

I was just in time: he was already on his horse, his attendants on theirs behind him, crossing the courtyard toward the gatehouse. Fortune favoured me, for Father was nowhere to be seen.

When Sir Andrew saw me, he at once dismounted and strode over. The others remained at a respectful distance. Reaching me, he removed his hat, a wide, floppy thing with an ostrich feather, and bowed. "Lady Margaret," he said.

"I didn't know you were to depart so soon today."

"The earl knew my plans. I am needed in London."

I had only a moment before Father would appear. It was time to be direct. "I will marry you," I said.

Surprised, he caught his breath. His head tilted slightly and his eyes widened. Then he smiled. "I am honoured beyond expression."

I half smiled in return.

His smooth and tanned forehead wrinkled, and one dark eyebrow lifted. "I fear your father may not agree?"

"He will. Once he sees I want it."

He flicked the fingers of his gloved hand upward. "What if the stars say otherwise?"

The morning light was growing stronger, the long shadows receding. The sky was a cloudless blue, and the day promised to be as fair as the one before. "During the day, the stars are gone. We navigate alone," I told him.

His gaze shifted over my shoulder and became blank. Without turning, I knew Father had appeared.

Sir Andrew bowed to him, and then to me. He then strode to his horse, leaped onto it and started out of the courtyard, his attendants trailing after him. Right before entering the passage through the gatehouse, he turned back to me and lifted his hat in salute.

Father stood next to me, and we watched them go. Distantly, I heard the sound of the gate being lowered.

"I told him yes," I said, my eyes fixed on the gate they had all just disappeared through. "I said I would marry him. He spoke of it yesterday, during the hunt."

I turned to look at Father. His face was drawn, with strain lines around his dark eyes, yet there was a resigned look about him. He sighed. "Are you certain?"

"He's to become Lieutenant Governor of the North. A peerage will follow, at least a barony. I find him suitable."

All around us the courtyard was coming to life with the start of the new day. Two dogs ran past, barking, and servants were moving between the storerooms, the Great Hall and the kitchens. Laughter and male voices could be heard from the barracks.

"I will not deny that I would have you marry elsewhere," Father said at last. "But there are many who desire this match besides the king. Sir Andrew brought a letter from your Aunt Frances; she urges it as a consolation of the unity between the two branches of our family. And the man himself is not without merit. But there is much here that is unsaid."

It was strange to have more knowledge than my father, but not unpleasant. The feeling of importance was enjoyable. He wore the same clothes as yesterday, telling me he'd been up all night, most likely observing the heavens, or perhaps using his new astrolabe.

"What do the stars say of this?" I asked.

"Nothing of clarity, just indications that it is not yet for us to know. But, as I said, it is a time of change — for all of us."

4

Father sent a fast messenger after Sir Andrew with a letter to the king approving the match. It was a week before one arrived back from the Privy Council in the king's name, approving the marriage and endorsing the plan for us to reside at Skipton Castle. Another letter came with it, from Sir Andrew, telling me he'd been given permission to select from the royal robes and jewels apparel fitting for our wedding. He would send them on to me at Skipton, along with his own household furnishings for the wing where we would reside.

"There is much to do!" I told Father. "The east wing at Skipton must be made ready. The rest of the castle will have to be prepared for the many guests, with other lodgings found in the town. And the wedding must be spectacular, as Jane's was. We should leave immediately for Skipton!"

He turned away, his shoulders hunching. "I don't know if I can —" he began.

But I seized his shoulders and whirled him around to me. "Yes, you can return there!" I said loudly. "We must return to life, Father. It's our family seat, and where we belong."

He had refused to allow his eyes to meet mine, but now they did. "Yes, we will go," he said after a moment. "It's time for you to take your place in the world." But his sombre mood hadn't improved at all.

Spring was much more advanced in Skipton, which I should have expected, it being farther south, in the centre of England. Unexpected also was how different the castle felt, less austere and more connected to life than the one at Brougham; the bustling town came right up to the castle's gate. I hadn't remembered how much more compact and homelike it was than Brougham, and every part of the building looked polished and ornate, with flowing curves and turns instead of solid blocks and sharp angles. The long eastern wing built for my mother had the look and feel of a luxurious modern mansion.

Although the castle had been overseen by relatives since our departure, the new wing had remained unused, frozen in time when my mother died. Untouched also was her clothing, which I found neatly arranged in the large carved oak chest in what had been her bedroom.

I had the gowns removed and spread out on the bed, hoping they would conjure her memory back for me. There were numerous elegant ones of velvet, satin and damask. Some were crimson, purple or gold, but most were the rich black that only the most expensive dyes could create. Some were lavishly embroidered, while others had lace or gold and silver trimmings, or brightly coloured undersleeves.

As I ran my fingers over them, I noted with surprise how pristine they were. But then I remembered that many of them had been made for her within the year before her death. Much had changed for us in that time, shortly before old King Henry had died. My mother, after years of melancholy and seclusion, had wanted the company of others again. After years at Brougham, we had returned to Skipton. There had been a burst of banquets, guests and visits, including to the court in London, and to Aunt Frances's home Bradgate. It had been then that several London merchants and dressmakers had arrived at Skipton, with wagonloads of riches, including the gowns.

There had been another change too, at that time: I no longer slept in my mother's bedroom, as I had in the earlier years there, and later when we'd moved to Brougham. The nursery, directly above her room, had been refitted for me. I had occupied it before, but after the death of my second brother, it had been closed, and I'd started sharing a room with Mother, and Father had moved into the lord's room in the older part of the castle. But when we'd returned, they had both shared their room again, and did so until the onset of her final illness, when the physicians had insisted he sleep elsewhere.

None of them ever found the cause of that illness, which had started in the late summer. All attempted remedies had been useless. A strange lethargy had crept over her, a disinterest in life at odds with her new-found vitality, yet different from the melancholy of the preceding years. There were some signs in the body — urine running red from time to time, vague aches, abhorrence of certain foods — but what I remembered most was the slowing, first of her speech, and then of her gestures and movements. Throughout the autumn she'd drifted away from us, in the final weeks simply lying upon her bed, not responding with even so much as a twitch of her face when addressed by Father, myself, her women, or any of the physicians. And then, in November, she had died.

The bed before me, still with the same hangings and covers of crimson damask and cloth of gold and silver, was the one she had died in. The bed certainly would have to be removed from the room when Sir Andrew and I occupied it. But the dresses might be a different matter. I felt the smoothness of the satins and lushness of the velvets. They'd been designed to impress and stand out even at court. They were not out of style and could easily be adjusted to fit me. Black suited me as well as it had my mother.

On the evening of our first day at Skipton, I supped alone with Father. The trip from Brougham had barely tired him, and our arrival at Skipton hadn't brought down the melancholy that always hovered over him. On the contrary, he appeared more alert and engaged than at Brougham, and he'd managed to organise the staff with a brisk competence that I'd overheard several of the stewards commenting admiringly on.

We were eating in the day room in the old part of the castle, the room between his and the one I would use until my marriage. But the banquet hall was near enough for the rest of the household to be heard at supper, everyone adjusting to the new residence after the uprooting from Brougham. They could almost be seen as well, since the main castle rooms were all arranged around a compact centre court, with large windows and doors opening into it.

"Everything here feels so much closer than at Brougham," I remarked to Father as we finished. "Even the new wing doesn't feel so far away, despite its length."

"That was why your mother preferred Brougham. She came to find the close proximity of others intolerable."

Casually, Father lifted his silver wine cup to his lips, but the look in his eyes as they fixed on my face was anything but casual.

"Why?" I asked, aware that this was the very question he had intended to provoke.

He set his wine cup down on the table, but his fingers remained wrapped around it. "Eleanor feared being poisoned." The shock that ran through my body undoubtedly showed on my face, but he ignored it and went on. "She was convinced your brothers had been poisoned, and that she too was being targeted."

I was aghast, not only at what he had just said, but at how he had said it, the mildness of his tone almost mocking the brutality of his words. As I stared across at him, I understood that he had been planning to tell me this since before we had left Brougham.

He drank from the cup again and set it down, his fingers once more lingering on it. "Here, there were too many people about. It was too difficult to control the comings and goings in and out of the castle. At Brougham she felt safer."

Servants appeared to clear away the plates from the final course we'd just finished. Grateful for the momentary respite, I looked down at the table. In the distance I could hear the boisterous voices in the banquet hall.

Memories crowded in on me, all now with horrible new significance: my mother eating alone with me in her rooms at Brougham, sometimes preparing the food right there. The incessant questioning of her women over the presence of any strangers. Her face turning pale with fear whenever she received seemingly trivial messages.

Before me, a servant was lifting away a plate, the contents of which I had just consumed with so little thought I could barely remember that it had been a honey-sweetened custard. *She feared being poisoned.* What would it have been like to view every morsel placed before you as possibly lethal? For a countess, eating was a ritual, a display before others. How unendurable would it have been to have sat on a dais before a crowded hall, not knowing whether each bite of food would cause one's demise?

Father finished his wine and handed his cup to a servant, and another took the remaining plates and left. I watched them go with despair, dreading the inevitable continuation of the conversation.

"Why did she fear it?" I finally managed to ask. "Why would someone have wanted to kill her?"

But as soon as the questions had passed my lips, I knew the answer. It was no surprise when he replied, "Because of her royal lineage. A son of hers could have become king."

"Was it true?" My voice was barely a whisper. "Did someone want her to die?"

"She was certain of it." Father leaned back in his chair, the first sign of his weariness. "Eleanor had already borne two sons, quickly conceived and easily birthed, excellent signs that there'd be more. Given the trouble Tudors tend to have with producing sons, this was exceptional — and threatening, she believed: she'd seen both of her brothers sicken and die. The second death in particular had aroused suspicions. The boy had lived to age eleven and had been created Earl of Lincoln by King Henry, a sign that he was favoured to succeed to the throne. The king's second wife, Madam Boleyn, had just given birth to a daughter instead of the expected son, and it had seemed that Henry was destined not to have one. When the little earl died, many darkly blamed Madam Boleyn. But there were others who saw how it benefitted the king's other nephew."

"My cousin James," I said weakly. "The King of Scotland." For a moment, I thought I would faint. I clutched the arm of my chair for support. The Scots were said to be an unruly and troublesome people. Not long ago, they had warred with England over the king's religious changes.

Father continued, "As the son of Henry's older sister, many, including James, saw him as the rightful heir to the English throne. But he also knew that King Henry did not favour him. And from your mother, there was the added threat of a competing claim from the north, rooted in the old religion, where James had hopes of influence. Whatever his true religious beliefs, he boldly announced his adherence to the ways of Rome, and opposition to his uncle's break with the Pope. It led to war, which was disastrous for him."

"He died during the war, did he not?"

"Afterward, on the heels of a terrible defeat. That was eleven years ago, in 1542."

"It was good that he died," I said bitterly. "A great relief for my mother."

"No. His death created another threat. He left one child, an infant daughter: Mary, now Queen of Scots. Her mother, now regent, is from a very powerful French family, the Guise. Eleanor suspected she had reason to fear them, even more than she had feared James, for with his death there was no longer the possibility of a male heir from the line of Scotland — or Guise. Mary Queen of Scots' only chance of succession to the English throne was in the absence of any male heir — which Eleanor still had the possibility of producing."

Another memory suddenly rearranged itself with stark clarity. "That was why she slept alone for years."

"She believed that if she appeared not to be able to have more children, she was safe. But she still feared retaliation. The Guise were vengeful, as well as ambitious. And they were also frightened. Mary was sent to France for safety."

"Why were they vengeful?"

"The year before King James died, both of the sons borne to him and Mary of Guise died." He paused. "The deaths happened on the same day, but in different locations. Poison was suspected. And where would suspicions fall but on a family in which two other royal sons had previously met untimely deaths? Your brothers had died shortly before, one in 1539 and the other in 1540."

A silence followed as the full meaning of what he had just said impressed itself upon me. It was interrupted by a burst of voices from outside in the courtyard. From the window I saw that the door to the banquet hall had opened, and members of the household were spilling out and down the wide stone steps into the courtyard. Several of the men still wore the Clifford livery they had worn during the trip from Brougham. Mindlessly, I stared out the window at them, trying to comprehend what Father had just told me.

"I didn't kill those princes," he said quietly. "Neither did Eleanor. But my father was a proud, ambitious man, with a violence in him." A touch of hardness now appeared on his face.

"Did he —" I started to ask, but he held up his hand.

"Do not ask it, Margaret. Some questions are better left unvoiced, and this is one of them. He died the following year. Vengeance again? Who is to say? But he was ambitious, and he let others know it. Securing the marriage of his son to the king's niece was a great coup for him, and he had hopes for the match. The building of the new wing here made that clear. And Eleanor was not averse to these ambitions: she shared them herself, and from the time of her brother's death, they had become more pronounced. She saw that if she had one boy who lived to be an adult, the throne might be his. She also saw the power of the north, very different from the south of England and steeped in the history of the Plantagenets, from whom both our families descend. It was a power that could be harnessed, and lead to the throne. Even after the king's third wife finally gave him an heir, everyone doubted there would be another."

There was a knock on one of the doors, and Father called for them to enter. It creaked open to reveal Mrs Brograve, as robust as ever, despite the trip from Brougham, during which she'd ridden her horse with valiant enthusiasm. Behind her, my three women hovered in the doorway, all looking pale and exhausted from the trip.

"Little swan," Mrs Brograve began, "do you want your mother's dresses taken —"

"I'll decide later," I interrupted. Mentioning them to Father at that moment would have been brutally inconsiderate. I waved her away, telling her to send my women to bed. "I'll need only you to attend me later," I said.

The image of those luxurious gowns danced in my head as she left. They had represented a time of new hopes: something had changed for my mother. "Why did my mother return to Skipton? What made her overcome her fears?"

"After the king named her in the succession, Eleanor's ambitions surfaced again."

Outside, most of the crowd was gone from the courtyard. Two lingering voices were heard in distant conversation, but they soon trailed off.

Finally, I said, "But she died."

"Yes. She died."

"And they couldn't find out what her illness was."

"She said nothing. She voiced no fears. She'd lost face before by showing her fears. She wouldn't do it again."

Suddenly, Father seemed to collapse. He leaned forward on the table and ran a hand over his face. "Beware of overreaching ambition, now, Margaret! Sir Andrew and his brother have ambitions, and they see the power of the north. They also see the influence of religion and understand that it can be manipulated to the advantage of those seeking power. You must guard against it. I should have told you this earlier, before Sir Andrew came to Brougham. Perhaps it would have influenced your decision in the matter of this marriage. It still can. It's not too late for you to change your mind."

In the moment that followed, the silence was overwhelming. Resentment and determination stirred within me. Father's choosing to tell me the sad and frightening tale he had, right at this time, was an attempt to dissuade me from the path I had chosen as Sir Andrew's wife. But the past, and my mother's fate, had nothing to do with me. Besides, it was clear to me that whatever possible dangers might lie ahead because of my own claim to the throne would be minimised by marriage to a powerful and politically savvy man with ties to the government, the court, and the king. In the end, my mother's marriage into an ancient and noble family hadn't protected her at all.

I was about to say so, but stopped. Father's journey through his past had clearly been difficult for him, and to follow it with such an observation would have been cruel. Instead, I said quietly, "I will marry Sir Andrew, as planned."

I stood up, went around to him, and lightly kissed his head. "Goodnight, Father. Everything will be well, you'll see."

But the look in his eyes as he turned them up to me showed he disagreed.

Later, in my room, I told Mrs Brograve, "My mother's gowns should be packed away again. It would be too much of a painful reminder for my father to see me wearing them. Don't throw them out or give them away, because in the future I may feel differently about them. But for now, just store them."

5

The next morning, sixteen of Sir Andrew's servants arrived from London with three wagons overflowing with bundles: for me, for our wedding, and to furnish our suite of rooms. Their arrival created a stir, as many members of the household rushed out into the wide outer courtyard, hoping to catch a glimpse of the treasures. From the windows of the long gallery, I watched as the grooms directed the wagons to the main entrance of the new wing. Giddy excitement came over me as I remembered the splendid gifts I'd received at Brougham, and I started hurrying off to unpack these new ones. But halfway through the gallery I stopped as I caught sight of the portrait of my mother that completely dominated one section of wall, separated from the other portraits of several generations of the Clifford family.

It felt as though I were seeing it for the first time, for when I'd lived at Skipton as a child, I'd had no cause to dwell on it. It was large, but half size, showing her elegantly dressed with a pearl collar and strands of pearls entwined in her elaborately arranged brown hair. Most striking was the look in her hazel eyes, which shone with pride and happiness. Certainly, it had been painted during her first years at Skipton, as the mother of three children, including two prized little boys.

The story my father had told me the previous evening seemed nearly unbelievable when faced with an image of such radiant self-assurance. Something terrible must have happened to turn her into the sad and withdrawn creature she had become. With a little shudder, I turned away, deciding it best to leave behind the troubles of the past. My mother's memory, and royal legacy, would best be honoured by my succeeding where her ambitions had failed. Sir Andrew was precisely the man to help me fulfil them. Fortune had favoured me by bringing him to my door.

His gifts were unloaded and brought into a large room in the new wing, where we unpacked and inventoried them. They were nothing short of breathtaking in their richness and beauty. There was handsome, intricately carved furniture; cassocks of black velvet, embroidered with gold; tapestries and rich velvet hangings and coverlets, and fine sheets and linen. Three cupboards were full of expensive plate, jewelled cups, and gold and silver bowls and spoons. Numerous chests held satin and velvet clothing, four sets for each of us, as well as velvet hats with ostrich feathers. Several coffers held rings, bracelets, necklaces and brooches, all intricately designed. Other coffers were full of gold and silver coins. Finally, there were numerous velvet-covered dog collars, for greyhounds.

Father picked up a collar and half-smiled. "He favours the hunt, I see," he said.

He had remained silent while the gifts had been unpacked, a sharp contrast to Mrs Brograve and my women, who had chattered excitedly, and Sir Andrew's servants, who had thoroughly enjoyed the women's admiration of their master's bounty.

"He went hawking with us at Brougham," I reminded my father.

"Greyhounds are different. They use speed rather than accuracy of perception." He put down the collar. "Sir Andrew hopes to make good use of the red deer on our estates." His tone was flat; he seemed resigned to my imminent marriage. Whatever his concerns, he must have seen there would be advantages to it.

The inventories were completed, and the gifts were locked into their cupboards, chests and coffers. It was agreed that we would hold those keys, while Sir Andrew's men would hold the key to the room they would be locked in.

Father went to take the keys we were to have, but I grabbed them first. "I'll take charge of them," I said grandly.

He stared at me, affronted. The room went quiet, everyone observing our discord. *They are always watching us*, I thought with unusual annoyance. I hadn't intended it to be so, but it now felt especially important that I win, especially in front of Sir Andrew's men. The outcome would certainly be reported to him.

Father shook his head. "The responsibility is too great. You aren't used to it. Give them to me."

He seemed indifferent to the audience around us, but I was keenly aware of it. Usually I liked the attention, but this time there was more at stake. My hands tightened around the keys. "No. It is now my place to hold them."

Without warning, his mild expression burst into one of anger. "You haven't yet the experience to protect what is yours!" he shouted. "You must always protect what is yours, for there will be many who will try to take it from you. Daughter, are you truly ready to do that?"

The vehemence in his voice was shocking, disproportionate to the argument. He was clearly talking about my birthright and royal inheritance rather than the treasures in the room.

"Yes," I answered.

"I fear you are not!"

His anger was rooted in fear, fear for me. To challenge him further would only provoke it more; I needed a different approach. "I am," I said, stepping forward and wrapping my arms around his shoulders and neck. "For I know you are always there to help me."

A murmur of fond approval ran through the room, and I thought they might even all break into applause. Father's shoulders relaxed as the tension left them, and his arms lifted up and encircled me. But I still clutched the keys tightly.

We dined in the banquet hall, the steward finding places for Sir Andrew's men, who were to remain with us permanently. Afterward, Mrs Brograve came to me in my room and told me one of them wished to speak with me.

"Where is he?"

"In the Day Room."

"Is my father there?"

"No, he is in the gatehouse meeting with townsfolk."

The man bowed when I entered; he was the one I had first encountered unpacking Sir Andrew's gifts at Brougham. He was short and slender, and had mild features that were pleasant but nondescript. His age was impossible to tell; he could have been anywhere between twenty and forty. His name, he said, was Alexander Harrison.

"Sir Andrew told me to deliver this to you directly." From inside his doublet he produced a letter.

I broke the seal, opened it and read:

My Lady Margaret,

Urgent matters of the utmost importance to the state as well as us delay me in London. My expectation is they will shortly be resolved and allow me to join you. In my absence, you can rely on my servant Harrison. He has been with me for many years and I trust him thoroughly. Any message he presents to you should be trusted as though directly spoken by me, and you can direct such to me through him as well; I will receive it faster than any letter. Meanwhile, rest assured I suffer this delay in joining you with much regret. Harrison has a small gift I wish you to receive as though from my own hands. He also has another message for you.

A.D.

Excitement nearly caused my hands to tremble. How different my life was from only a month ago!

Mrs Brograve was hovering behind me, her curiosity palpable. I dismissed her. "I wish to take my exercise in the long gallery, and Mr Harrison will keep me company," I said. Seeing her stare and begin to protest, I added, "You can never keep up with me. Mr Harrison will be a more suitable companion." She said nothing, but I was sure her eyes were fixed on my back as the door closed behind us.

The watchful eyes of my Clifford forebears looked down on us as we began to walk the length of the gallery. "Mr Harrison, I find Sir Andrew's letter cryptic. How is it possible for a spoken message to reach him before a letter?"

"Between here and London, Sir Andrew has friends whose interests are compatible with his. They exert themselves with speed to do his bidding. Many served under him in the wars." He withdrew a small, silk-wrapped package from inside his doublet and handed it to me.

Inside the silk was an eagle-shaped golden brooch, sprinkled with diamonds. The fine jewels inventoried earlier paled in comparison. As I held it up, it gleamed in the sunlight streaming through the window.

"Sir Andrew wishes to remind you he promised you an eagle, at Brougham," Mr Harrison said.

"Indeed, I remember," I said, delighted with the new gift.

"He wonders if you are aware that in hunting, the eagle is only used by the highest level of royalty."

My hand closed around the brooch. I stopped walking and faced him, attempting to convey with my expression that the suggestiveness of the remark had not been lost on me. "Sir Andrew wrote that you have another message for me. Why did he not simply write it?"

"My lady, some things are best not written."

"Such as?"

"The succession to the throne is to be altered. It is this matter that detains Sir Andrew in London."

The news was so startling the letter dropped from my fingers and fluttered to the floor. But I still held the brooch tightly.

"Perhaps it would be best if I disposed of this," Mr Harrison suggested as he picked up the letter. "Now that you've read it." He folded it and put it back inside his doublet. "The news surprises you?"

"At Brougham, Sir Andrew alluded to the possibility of it. But I didn't expect it so soon."

"The king has considered it for months, and with increasing concern as his illness has worsened. He recognises he may not live long enough for a male heir of his own body. He also views the succession of his sister Mary with abhorrence because of her beliefs. Her illegitimacy, and that of his sister Elizabeth, troubles him further. He has decided to bar both from succeeding. Instead, upon his death without heir, the crown will go to any male child borne to his cousins the Lady Frances, her daughters Jane, Catherine or Mary — or you."

His words, quiet yet so monumental, swirled around me. The entire gallery seemed to spin. I caught my breath, steadying myself. Looking up, I saw we had stopped directly beneath the portrait of my grandfather, the first Earl of Cumberland.

Mildly, Mr Harrison recited, "Henry Clifford. First Earl of Cumberland. Fifteenth Lord Clifford. Eleventh Baron of

Westmoreland. Second Baron Vesci. Related to the house of Tudor through his mother Anne St Leger, half-first cousin to King Henry VII, but on the non-royal side. Grew up at court with Prince Henry." For the first time, tiny notes of emotion came into his voice. "Oh, how that must have rankled, being the less important cousin, placed by birth a few steps from the throne. The reports are of a wild young man, violent and quarrelsome. He dressed himself and his horse in cloth of gold. But King Henry favoured him." He turned his small brown eyes to me and laughed softly, an oddly charming sound. "I am gifted in remembering what I learn, Lady Margaret. It is one reason why Sir Andrew prizes my attendance, and why my messages are so accurate. But we digress from the matter of importance."

"How ill is the king?" I asked.

"Physicians from the continent have privately told my lord Duke that he has a year to live, at most. Not so long, but perhaps long enough for the king to see the birth of a son: to the Lady Jane, or to you. No one expects Frances Grey to have another child." He paused. "That son would be king. The mother would be regent."

Regent. Regent for my son, the king. My fingers tightened around the brooch. "My marriage must be concluded soon."

"My lord Duke and Sir Andrew hold the king's favour more than any others. Nothing would please him more than to see a Dudley on the throne. He trusts that his legacy of religious change would be preserved that way."

"What remains for the change to be accomplished?" I whispered.

"Judges have already been instructed to draw up the official document. It will then be presented to the Privy Council to approve. They, the nobility at court, and anyone else of importance will be asked to sign it and swear to uphold it. In September, the new succession will be ratified by Parliament." He waited a moment, as though searching for the right words. Then he said, "The king has hopes that by then there will at least be signs of a possible child."

September. It was already June. Our marriage needed to happen at the earliest possible moment. "Will the judges agree to the changes? And will everyone else approve them?"

"Sir Andrew thinks so. But he must remain in London until it is accomplished."

"His brother relies on his support."

Mr Harrison hesitated. "Yes. But he also needs to remain visible before such a group of dignitaries. If they adjust easily to these changes, they might be inclined to adjust to others, at some future point." He leaned toward me. "Sir Andrew said he mentioned to you at Brougham that Frances and Henry Grey's marriage might be questioned due to precontract. Their children could be seen as illegitimate. Which would move you closer in the succession, child or not. But the presence of a male child of Tudor lineage would be an enormous advantage."

I stared up at my grandfather's portrait. It felt as if his eyes locked directly upon me. His ambitions must have soared with the births of my two brothers, only to be cruelly dashed when they died. Such desperate unfulfillment could easily have sharpened into a deadly exchange of infanticide and murder in a struggle for pre-eminence in the succession.

Farther down the gallery was the portrait of my mother, gentler and happier. It was entirely possible she had succumbed to nothing more than fear and illness, and that the series of deaths had been nothing more than physical weakness and susceptibility to the whims of fate. A man like my grandfather would have found it easier to believe in a mortal opponent, then an omnipotent one.

An opportunity was being presented to me. I would not let fear deter me, nor the mistakes, misfortunes or imaginings of those before me.

"But my Aunt Frances herself still has a claim?" I asked.

"Yes, but as I said, it is unlikely she will ever bear another child. And should it be decided that her daughters are illegitimate, she would be childless, not a very attractive prospect for the succession. Time will also allow other plans to unfold. Sir Andrew hopes to establish the success of your marriage and new positions of power and influence in the north. The match promises much: you bring a claim to the throne and other lineage, and an immense territorial inheritance. He brings great wealth, shrewdly gained over a lifetime and kept accessible and useable, in jewels and cash — which yours is not. It will allow the two of you to use your assets to position yourselves as prominent figures not just in the north, but in the entire country. You are poised on the verge of great success."

It was a compelling vision of the future. "My inheritance will be large. My father shows no inclination to marry again; he feels it would dishonour my mother. Although as a woman I cannot inherit the earldom, the Clifford, Westmoreland and Vesci titles will someday be mine. My husband can be granted them in my right. Any son of ours could inherit the earldom."

"As well as the throne."

Behind us, at the far end of the gallery, the doors opened and my women appeared. The time remaining for our conversation would be brief.

"Could I succeed to the throne myself?"

Mr Harrison spoke quickly. "Yes — with this marriage. Perhaps later rather than sooner. Much depends on how long the king lives. Sir Andrew brings skill, a network of allies at court, diplomatic ability, and recognised and admired military service against both France and Scotland. Your Aunt Frances's husband hasn't the same advantages: he is viewed mainly as a religious Reformer and socialite." His expression grew derisive. "And Jane's husband Guildford will never amount to anything."

6

That evening, Father told me he wished me to accompany him the next day to Bolton Priory. "We have been absent owners during our years at Brougham, despite our having had very good stewards caring for it. The rents have been strong, and the mill and the farms have done excellently, as well as they did when the monks were there. It is one of our most valuable properties." His lips pressed into a wry half-smile. "Loot, I should say."

I looked at him inquisitively. "Loot?"

"One of the more practical sides of King Henry's break with Rome was the dissolution of the monasteries. The king took them and sold them to replenish his treasury, or gifted them as rewards to his friends. Our family received Bolton Priory and its properties, and many of those of Roche Abbey. There were some nominal payments, but mostly they were gifts." He raised his eyebrows. "Some may see these gains as loot. Others do not, especially those with religious beliefs at odds with Rome. Many of the reformed party became extremely wealthy this way. It is true that your grandfather was not a Reformer. But had he not benefitted from the redistribution the way others did, they would have surpassed him in wealth and position. And my father, as I've explained to you, had ambitions."

The following morning was fine, good for an excursion. Shortly after breakfast, we rode out with a small group of Father's gentlemen and Mrs Brograve. The summer solstice had just passed, and the low, rolling landscape on the way was a lush green, the breezes fragrant.

I had hazy memories of the priory, but when we arrived, it felt even less familiar to me than Skipton Castle had. Many of the buildings had been dismantled, stripped of their lead roofs and ornate interiors, which had been sold for profit. Others were gone completely, their stone blocks taken for use elsewhere, while some stood half demolished, mournful relics of the centuries when the priory had flourished. Most shocking was the church, half of which had been destroyed, with only the skeletal outer walls still standing. The other side was intact, and still used as a church. But other buildings had been repurposed as homes, and the mill and farming enterprises of the priory were still functioning as successfully as ever.

After inspecting the properties and visiting the tenants, who made much ado about greeting us, we retired to the gatehouse. The previous day Father had sent a message ahead to the caretakers that we would be there for dinner.

The three-storey stone gatehouse had spacious and comfortable rooms; Father and I dined together in an upstairs one, Mrs Brograve and the gentlemen below. As we sat down, Father said, "This gatehouse was much favoured by your mother as a retreat from Skipton, when she wanted a change of scene. Even before the priory was dissolved, she had used it: the monks kept it comfortably furnished for distinguished guests. The Clifford family had traditionally supported the priory, and the prior was always happy to make it available. Eleanor liked it. Too much so, perhaps. It led her into danger here."

Even now, a sense of peace hung about the priory. It was hard to imagine any trouble occurring here. "What kind of danger could have touched her here, among the gentle monks and religious people?"

"A rebellion of the people of the north in 1536, in protest of the king's religious changes. It came to be known as the Pilgrimage of Grace; it was widespread and very nearly successful. Ours was one of only three of the great families of the north who remained loyal to the king. Skipton Castle was besieged while your mother and infant brother, and her women, were here at Bolton. The rebels discovered them here and attempted to use them as hostages to gain control of the castle. Disaster was averted by the bravery of one knight, who under cover of darkness secretly escorted them back."

The gatehouse wasn't a fortress, so there had been nothing to hold the rebels at bay. Most likely they had come close to the walls. I could imagine my mother sitting in the room we were in, probably able to hear gruff and arguing voices directly below the window.

"Eleanor knew that as the niece of the king, no one would dare to touch her or our son," Father went on. "But afterward the episode affected her enormously by having impressed on her the power of the people of the north, and their religion. It was then that she began to distance herself from the Reformers. We conformed with the changes only so far as we needed to. Our son, she felt, could become a great leader of the north, whom the throne might in time come to. At that time the late King Henry still had no son."

The servants had been setting out the first course of fruit, meat pie, boiled meats and bread, and cups of wine were placed before us. When they left, Father began to eat, but I did not, instead sitting silently across from him until he finally noticed.

"You have no appetite?" he asked.

"I see now that you brought me here today for a reason," I said accusingly. "Was it to once more impress upon me the dangers of ambition?"

He didn't deny it. His reply was brutally frank. "More, the dangers of how religion can be manipulated to personal advantage. I wanted you to see the wealth tied to the issue, even where it has been to our family's advantage. I've had news that the king is ill. If the Lady Mary succeeds as queen, it is widely believed that she will seek to return to the Catholic Church everything that was taken from the monasteries. There are some who stand to lose fortunes."

"Such as my Grey cousins? And the Dudleys?"

Father inclined his head. "Your cousin the king has had nothing but the loftiest of ideas and religious goals. It is those around him who have had more mercenary concerns. They will try very hard to protect what they have."

"They may succeed."

"Indeed, they may. But we must try to protect ourselves, should they not. Rumours have reached me from London about possible changes. Apparently, the king's illness is severe. And the stars tell of a time of great turbulence, with uncertain outcomes."

The rumours were confirmed later in the week with the arrival of official letters from the king and the Privy Council. Father summoned me to his office. But on the way there in an otherwise empty corridor, Mr Harrison stepped in front of me and drew me aside. "It is done," he whispered. "The succession has been changed. Not quite as we expected, but still to our advantage. Frances Grey has been overstepped and is not named. Jane succeeds outright, if there is no male heir. You are named following her sisters, for your male heirs to succeed." Someone approached behind us, and he disappeared quickly through a side door.

Father had the letters spread out on a table before him. He indicated for me to sit on the other side.

I feigned curiosity. "Mrs Brograve told me you have official letters from the king and the Privy Council?"

"And others." He folded his hands on the table, interlocking his fingers, and told me the news. All the while he watched me intently; clearly, he had suspicions I might already know. "Your position is improved," he concluded.

Trying my best to sound sincere, I replied, "I doubt anything will come of it."

"Clearly, this was known before Sir Andrew approached you. But he didn't say so to me. His presentation was that we would preserve the family unity with two Dudley marriages, which would aid us all should the Lady Mary succeed and seek a Spanish marriage. The plan held advantages for us; it still does. But there was obviously deceit regarding this change. One of my friends in London writes that the king has been considering this for months." He shuffled the other letters and picked one up. "He also writes that the king is dying. The new will has been sworn to by everyone of importance in London, more than a hundred of the nobility, council, bishops and the London aldermen. But it still must be ratified by Parliament in September. There are some who pray the king will live long enough for that to happen. There are others who pray he will not."

I rose to leave. Better for me to say nothing, so I wouldn't let slip that I knew more than he did.

He gestured to another letter. "From Sir Andrew," he said. "He writes that he is no longer needed in London, and that he should be here within a few days. The king, he says, desires that your marriage be concluded with all haste."

The news brought a smile to my lips; I was not being overlooked amidst all the changes. "As do I," I could not resist saying. "As you say, my position has improved. Sir Andrew is just the man to make the most of this opportunity." I turned to leave. "There is much to prepare for the wedding. I'd best get about it, if he is to arrive shortly. He'll want no delay!"

"Margaret," Father said sternly, causing me to turn back around to face him. He looked at me as though I troubled him. "Your cousin is dying. He may not even see sixteen years of age. Does this really leave you so unaffected?"

Stung, anger leaped up in me. "Of course it affects me!" I protested. "It is tragic. But, Father, I only met him once. How much can you expect me to grieve?"

Wordlessly, he looked down at the letters before him. I felt unpleasant and greedy.

"Your rebuke is intolerable, Father!" I exclaimed, all the tension of the past weeks finally overflowing. "If I am selfish, who has made me so? For years you have kept me locked away from the world at Brougham, while you nursed your grief and disappointment. Now, you resent my chance of happiness. You have done nothing but attempt to cloud it and frighten me with stories of the past. It is not I who is selfish, but you!" I turned and ran out before he could see my tears.

The ministrations of my women, if they saw me so distressed, would have been unbearable, so I lingered in the corridor, leaning against the wall. My tears stopped, and gradually I managed to push back the ugly feelings of inadequacy and selfishness Father had provoked.

Once again, Mr Harrison appeared directly in front of me, as though from nowhere. He handed me a handkerchief, and I blew my nose.

"Is Sir Andrew on his way?" I asked.

"His departure is imminent. He should be here within days."

"Tell him to hurry."

A week later, he still hadn't arrived. The weather had been glorious — sweet-smelling summer days with soft breezes. I walked in the parklands near the castle with my women and tried to absorb the peace and beauty. But the uncertainty of the delay was arduous. Time and again I retreated to my room and took out the little golden eagle brooch and held it, drawing strength from the glorious future it promised.

One day I finally managed to shake off my women and Mrs Brograve and found Mr Harrison. "What delays Sir Andrew? I had expected him by now."

"The king is very ill. No one expects him to live until September. Steps must be taken to see that his will and device for the succession remains unchallenged. Support is being sought from the French king, who does not want to see Spanish influence here. Sir Andrew must remain with his brother at this time. The duke may send him to France to negotiate."

More days passed as I remained poised in uncertainty, holding fear at bay, clutching my eagle brooch. I maintained a perfect politeness with Father, never mentioning what might be happening in London. But with my women I was merciless: I berated them over small mistakes, I threw clothes on the floor, made incessant demands and assigned foolish chores and errands. One time I actually raised my hand to slap Mrs Brograve, but her look of hurt and astonishment was enough to stop me. I threw myself down on my bed and buried my face in the pillows.

"Why have the little swan's feathers been so ruffled of late?" she asked.

"Don't call me that," I answered harshly. "Don't ever call me that again." But my voice was muffled by the pillows and I wasn't sure she heard me.

And then, one morning on our way to prayers, Mr Harrison caught my eye. Others, including Father, were about, and he dared not approach me, but he surreptitiously mouthed the word 'news'. Then, as we left the chapel, a messenger rode through the gatehouse into the outer courtyard. He spoke to a guard, who approached Father and whispered to him as the messenger dismounted, with his leather pouch of letters. Father beckoned to the messenger and hurried quickly into the castle with him as the guard led the exhausted horse to the stable.

Everyone in the household had stood watching, and an excited murmur rippled through them. There was no way for me to speak to Mr Harrison with so many people around, slowly making their way back inside for breakfast. A strange new feeling of calm and resignation took hold of me: there was nothing to do but wait. Slowly and serenely, I walked ahead of my women across the courtyard and up the grand steps to the front door of the castle. Just as I reached the door, the bells in Skipton church started ringing. Everyone stopped and looked back toward the town. Curiosity showed on every face except mine, and likely Mr Harrison's.

I was no farther than the inner courtyard when Father sent for me.

He was in his study, as he'd been the last time important letters had arrived from London. But whereas then he'd been seated, studious and pensive, with them on the table before him, this time he was standing tensely. He did not even ask me to sit.

"The king is dead," he said quietly. "In London, Jane has been proclaimed queen. But the Lady Mary has also declared herself queen, in Norfolk. Both sides are gathering forces." His eyes narrowed, and he half lifted a hand as though to ward off imminent danger. "It is dreadful, a return to the wars of the Plantagenets. The avoidance of this was behind King Henry's desperate quest for a son; those terrible times had been impressed on him by his father. The Tudors brought peace after years and years of one family warring for the throne."

"Surely it won't be so bad," I said. "The Duke of Northumberland has been at the centre of anything of importance in England for years, while the Lady Mary has been a recluse, far from court. She has no military or abilities as a leader. It can only be a matter of time until she is brought to heel."

Father looked at me strangely and seemed on the verge of saying something, but stopped. Then he strode over to the door and told the attendant waiting outside to assemble the household in the inner courtyard. When I started to leave, he stopped me, saying, "Stay. You will stand beside me when we tell them." There was coldness in his voice.

When everyone had been crowded into the courtyard, he and I emerged from the banquet hall onto the top of the stone staircase leading down to them. Our appearance caused a hush, even before the ushers signalled for silence. Just as Father was about to speak, a crow flew by overhead, shrieking. In the crowd, all heads turned toward it. Then everything was quiet, except for the distant mournful tolling of the church bell.

"Good people, I have just received sad news from London," Father announced. "Our young King Edward is no more."

There were some vocal responses to this, expressions of sadness, but none of surprise. Apparently, all had been aware of the king's failing health, having learned of it in that mysterious way news spread among the people.

Father continued, "After struggling valiantly with an illness that took hold of him earlier this year, he has now joined his father, King Henry, in heaven." He paused, drew a deep breath, and said, "Our new sovereign is Queen Jane."

A shocked silence greeted this proclamation. Then, from the back of the crowd, one voice burst out, "Jane?"

Other low voices in the back followed, confused and disapproving. Closer to us were the women and gentlemen of the household, who remained silent, but stared at us with blatant incredulity.

From the rear, someone called out, "Queen *Jane*? Who's Jane?"

Father answered, "Jane was cousin to King Edward, and great-granddaughter to King Henry VII. She is a lady of high virtue who was much esteemed by the late king."

The next voice held the sting of rebuke. "It's supposed to be the Lady Mary! Good King Henry's daughter!"

There was an immediate wave of agreeing voices in the back. Fear began to stir in me. I scanned the crowd for Sir Andrew's attendants, and saw them huddling together, off to one side, as though they had closed ranks for security. In the centre stood Mr Harrison, his face, as usual, without expression.

Other questions followed in rapid succession. What had happened to the Lady Mary? Had she been executed? Had she gone to Spain for protection by her relatives? And what of the king's other sister, the Lady Elizabeth? Wasn't the throne to go to her after the Lady Mary?

Father held up his hand, and an usher tapped his staff on the ground for silence. "Several weeks ago, the king changed his will," Father explained calmly. "The Lady Mary and Lady Elizabeth were both removed from the succession because they are not legitimate."

Again, it was from the rear that the first response came, a loud groan, followed by, "Oh, no! Not all *that* again!"

Other groans followed, and a voice cried, "Queen Catherine, Queen Anne — who cares who was the real queen? They're his daughters, aren't they? He said they were! And that's good enough for me!"

All around the courtyard were loud expressions of agreement. I noticed Mrs Brograve and my women joining in, nodding vigorously.

The protests continued, the jeering tones becoming more pronounced.

"For sure, the little king's throne should go to his sister, not to this Jane, whoever she is! I tell you, someone in London's up to no good!"

"It has a stink to it, if you ask me!"

"Mary's been cheated, thrown out like an old shoe!"

"Poor little thing, and her only brother not even cold in his grave!"

Again, Father raised his hand, and one of the ushers tapped his staff. Immediately, silence prevailed: no matter how strong the dissatisfaction, there was still respect for him.

With the utmost gravity, he said, "The Lady Mary has challenged the succession of Jane. She has proclaimed herself queen."

In the back, cheers of approval erupted. But Father stopped them at once, again lifting his hand. When he spoke, his voice was stern. "It is not for us to question the wisdom of the late king. Often matters are beyond our understanding. We must trust that his actions were divinely inspired. Tomorrow, at chapel, we will pray not only for the soul of King Edward, but for the new Queen Jane, and the Lady Mary also. And we will pray that the armies that are being formed by both sides do not come to battle." He turned slightly toward me. "I remind all of you that the king was cousin to my daughter, the Lady Margaret, who is Tudor through her mother, the Lady Eleanor. I ask you to be mindful of her loss, and the difficulty of her present position in being a close cousin to both Jane and Mary. The distress the rift within her family is causing her is great."

There was no response, no more calls or questions. This time, the silence that followed was respectful: Father had deftly shifted the crowd's focus away from their disapproval and reminded them of their personal loyalty to us. They had positions in our household, places that were hard to come by.

We turned and re-entered the banquet hall. Once inside, Father said to me, "What happened here will be the same all over England. It will be no easy matter for Queen Jane to hold her throne."

Members of the surrounding nobility and gentry, and their followers, began to arrive at the castle, all with sombre and troubled faces, seeking reassurance and advice from Father. Some of what he told them, I heard: he had hopes that the conflict would resolve before the north was drawn into it. Armies were being raised in the south, but not yet as far as York. The new government in London had requested he be prepared to enlist support if needed, and be ready to defend Skipton Castle against possible attack.

At dinner I was alarmed to notice the absence of nearly all of Sir Andrew's men. Mr Harrison was one of the few still present. Afterward I sought him out, taking advantage of Father's preoccupation with the new visitors. Mrs Brograve hesitated when I told her to send for him. "Little swan, is it wise for you to be seen talking to him? So far, not too many of the people here know Sir Andrew is the uncle of the new queen's husband —"

"Soon they will all know it!" I interrupted her. "You overstep! Now find him at once and have him meet me in the long gallery!"

Opposite the portrait wall, the gallery had several windows, all overlooking the spreading outer courtyard. I looked out of one as I waited, watching all the unusual comings and goings brought about by the news from London. Grooms were tending to horses, and servants stood about in little groups, talking amongst themselves. I doubted their conversation was about anything other than my relatives, and how we were now in conflict.

"They have power," said a whispery voice behind me. It was Mr Harrison, who I hadn't heard come in. He stepped beside me and waved toward the window. "Whoever underestimates the power of the common folk makes a mistake."

But I had no desire for thoughtful musings. "Where are your companions?"

"Gone. Sir Andrew sent orders for them to join him. He is charged with forming an army in Hertfordshire."

"The Lady Mary can't possibly win, can she?"

He avoided answering outright. Instead, he said, "It was a mistake for the duke not to take her prisoner before Edward died. It's clear now that she had full knowledge of what had happened in London, and was prepared. She was immediately proclaimed queen by the gentlemen of her household and has already been joined by a large number of knights and gentlemen from Norfolk and Suffolk. None of the great lords have rallied around her — yet. Or at least they hadn't when the last message was sent." He shrugged. "As of now, who knows? If the response among the people is the same as what we saw here, the other earls will take note of it, just as my Lord of Cumberland did this morning."

The suggestion that Father had been seeking the response of the household was surprising. "Do you really think he was trying to determine how they felt? Not just informing them of the king's death?"

"Oh, yes. He wanted you to see it also." He looked out the window. "Every lord learns to respect the power of the people. Who is it, after all, who make up the armies? And they tend to be less fickle than their leaders."

There was something ominous in the remark, and I felt that if I pursued it, I might hear things I didn't wish to. "Did Sir Andrew send any message for me?" I asked.

"No." The single word had a harsh and lonely ring to it.

"He told you to remain here?"

"Yes, which satisfies me. It is better to be somewhat removed from the centre of the situation, in the event that things don't turn out as planned." Our eyes met, then Mr Harrison quickly looked away. It was then that I understood that Queen Jane's cause was already lost.

Days of rumours followed, interspersed with long stretches of eerie silence. Then, York declared for Mary. Father assembled the household and did the same, to cheers and delighted cries. He then took the keys to Sir Andrew's treasures from me, confiscating everything in the name of Queen Mary. He also gathered all the gifts Sir Andrew had brought to Brougham, including the astrolabe, and put them in a chest in the new wing.

The next morning, Sir Andrew's remaining servants were gone, including Mr Harrison. He had stopped receiving any messages several days earlier, apparently right when the duke's support had begun to collapse. The lack of connection to his patron of years had affected him, and he had seemed to wither before my eyes.

Father, though, had been strengthened by the shifting of powers in the south. After messengers from London had arrived, he told me of Mary's complete victory. "Critical to Northumberland's collapse was his failure to remain in London. Jane flatly refused to allow her father to leave her, and so Northumberland had to lead the forces in the field. Without his dominating presence, the Privy Council turned to Mary: they had seen the growing support for her. In Cambridge, the duke — and his brother — gave up and acknowledged Mary as queen."

He then told me that Jane and her husband were imprisoned in the Tower of London. "They face charges of treason. There is a good chance both will be executed. Certainly, the Duke of Northumberland will be, and perhaps his brother and other sons with him. And Jane's father. But her mother and sisters should be able to avoid that fate, as should we. Hopefully the queen will understand the difficulty of the position we were in. But possibly not. There could be grave consequences for us because of our involvement. The queen may never trust us again."

Over the past few days, I had slowly adjusted to the vanishing of all my hopes and ambitions. I had vaguely assumed things would go back to the way they had been, with

Father and me returning to our sleepy life at Brougham. Only now did I realise the full extent of the danger we were in. Those days at Brougham were gone forever.

Fear grabbed at me, but anger drove it away. "Your studies of the heavens are worthless," I said with disdain. "Could not the stars have warned of this?"

"They did."

"Then why did you not act upon it?"

"I did, as much as I was able. They advised caution. And I was cautious, even if you were not. This could have gone either way. There were too many people, and too many fates and fortunes involved to predict a clear outcome."

"And what happens next?"

"Tonight, I will send the queen by fast messenger an explanatory account of our involvement, and a plea for understanding. Tomorrow, we leave to present ourselves in person at Framlingham Castle, where she has gathered her army."

"Where is that?"

"In East Anglia. The Lady Mary — *Queen* Mary — went there for the strong Catholic support, and to be near the coast if she needed to escape to the Low Countries. The duke sent five ships to prevent it, but the crews of all switched sides. News of these defections travelled quickly and made a huge impression. That was the beginning of the end for the duke."

Back in my room, I took out the gold and diamond eagle brooch, which I had held back from the gifts I'd given over to Father. The full extent of the debacle seemed too great to comprehend, and I felt a powerful desire to sleep. As I lay down on my bed, I was nearly overwhelmed with sadness as I thought of the loss of the peace and comfort of my years at Brougham. But I still held the brooch tightly in my hand.

7

To ensure speed, Father and I travelled with a much smaller entourage than had accompanied us from Brougham. Of the women, only Mrs Brograve came with us. News reached us along the way, sufficient for us to know not to expect the worst for ourselves: Jane's father had been released after only three days and was now back at Bradgate with Aunt Frances and Catherine and Mary. Sir Andrew had been brought to the Tower with his brother and nephews; an armed guard had been needed to protect them from angry crowds on the London streets. In a few weeks, all the conspirators would go on trial and be convicted. But it was likely only those the queen saw as most guilty would be executed, and the others eventually pardoned.

Other reports mentioned that Jane would be spared, and possibly her husband, but almost all said the duke was clearly doomed. None mentioned Sir Andrew at all, leaving me to wonder what his fate would be. I hoped it would not be the worst. I had barely spent one full day with him, yet I felt that I knew him. Certainly, I didn't love him, and I wasn't even sure I liked him. Yet the brief intersection of our lives had impressed me powerfully in ways I didn't fully understand. In no way did I feel responsible for the dire circumstances he now found himself in; if anything, anger would have been more appropriate, since he had tried to draw me in also. But I wasn't angry, and I knew that if he lost his life it would leave me sorely troubled. Hopefully, the queen would prove as merciful as she was said to be. There were indications she would be so to all but the most central of the conspirators, as they were now called.

Framlingham Castle looked even larger than either of our castles at Brougham or Skipton, its tall walls and battlements looming in the distance against a clear blue afternoon sky as we approached. Spread out around it was the camp of the huge army that had assembled in support of the cause. Its sheer size was a clear demonstration of Mr Harrison's whispery words at Skipton: *Whoever underestimates the power of the common folk makes a mistake.*

Father, riding just ahead of me, turned to the gentleman beside him and said, "It looks about ten thousand still here. Yesterday, the news was that the larger part was disbanded, around twenty thousand. This is what the queen will take into London with her." The land around us showed signs of having been occupied by that larger force: trampled grasses and abandoned tents.

The day was unusually clear; with the sun beating down on us as we crossed the wide empty space, we felt exposed and vulnerable. As we drew closer to the castle, some of the troops began to swarm toward us to see who we were. From the entrance gate, armed guards rode out to escort us in, forming lines on either side of us. Beyond them, soldiers continued to gather along the road, staring and pointing at us. I heard *Cumberland* repeated several times, and *from the north.*

One voice said, "That must be the other queen — Jane."

"Nope, she's in the Tower. Probably got no head on her shoulders anymore — this one's still got hers!"

Much guffawing followed. I stared ahead in disbelief and gripped the reins of my horse. But Mrs Brograve, riding beside me, cried out angrily, "Wretched fools, in Cumberland you'd be whipped for disrespect! The lady is Margaret Clifford, great-granddaughter to King Henry VII!"

Father silenced her with a look over his shoulder. Another voice called out, "So was that Jane! And look where that got her!"

The guards raised their weapons and aimed them at the men as a deterrent. At the head of the line the captain swiftly turned his horse around and rode back to them. "These are the honoured guests of Queen Mary!" he shouted.

We were past them now, but close enough to hear one final comment: "Well, how were we to know that? These Plantagenets have always been killing each other off."

"Not another word, or the queen will hear of it!" the captain ordered severely.

Ignoring him, a man called, "Sorry, lady! Any friend of Queen Mary's is a friend of ours!"

There were cries of affirmation as we rode off. I should have forced myself to look back at them and smile, but I found myself incapable of it. The captain rode up beside Father and said, "I'm sorry, my lord. These men got themselves worked up, expecting a battle that never happened. They don't come down from that so easily."

As we dismounted in the courtyard, Father said quietly, "All signs are good for us. She sent an honour guard out in greeting."

But his reassurance helped me little, and it was with the most extreme effort that I was holding stark terror at bay. The episode outside had been shocking, hinting at a violent world I had no experience of, one where a young woman's execution provoked laughter.

An usher came toward us. "The queen awaits you in the Great Hall," he said smoothly. "Please follow me."

I dreaded coming face to face with the queen. I had only one clear memory of her from the few times we had met before my mother had died, of a pretty, small woman meticulously applying herself to her needlework. That image was now expanded to monstrous proportions by the raw power I had seen outside. *Ten thousand men*, had been Father's words. *Twenty thousand already disbanded.* I remembered what Mr Harrison had said as well: *Every lord learns to respect the power of the people. Who is it, after all, who make up the armies?* Queen Mary, apparently, had learned the lesson well, but Jane had not.

Inside, the hall was packed. Sunlight streamed in through the windows, and torches had been lit in darker corners.

Abruptly, all the voices fell silent. I became aware of a sea of male faces, all turning toward us. Then, they separated, forming a long aisle, at the far end of which stood a small figure, indistinct except for the vivid red garment swathing it, a sharp contrast to the dull browns and greys surrounding us.

My legs felt as though they would buckle beneath me. Somehow, I managed to step forward beside Father, and we began to walk between the lines of silent, staring men, our entourage close behind us. Slowly, the red-clad figure came into focus, and I recognised my cousin Mary, now Queen of England.

She stood beside a table surrounded by men, advisors with whom she must have been conferring. All towered above her; she was even shorter than I'd remembered. But her face had barely aged, although six years had passed and she was now in her late thirties. I'd intended to lower my eyes out of respect when I approached, but I now felt compelled to do exactly the opposite; I couldn't look away. Mary had a pink complexion and pretty, balanced features. But there was also an oddness to her face, caused by the extreme fairness of her eyebrows, which were almost invisible. They contrasted sharply with her rich red hair, which showed in front of her French-style hood.

Her gaze remained fixed on us as we came to a stop a few feet before her, and sank to our knees. I could finally see her eyes, which were grey-blue.

"Mary, Queen of England," Father said firmly, bowing his head. I did and said the same, but in a much quieter voice, all I could manage.

"Welcome, Earl of Cumberland, and Cousin Margaret," she replied. Her voice was startling in its depth, more like a man's, and completely unexpected from one of such small and delicate stature. "If you would please rise."

Everyone stood; I felt as though I was floating upward.

"I have read your account of your unfortunate entanglement with the Dudleys," she said, loud enough for her voice to fill the entire hall. "I find it acceptable, with the ring of truth. I appreciate your frank acknowledgement of acting in accordance with the difficulty of circumstances. Praise God, Lord Clifford, that he protected you, and Lady Margaret."

"Thank you, Your Majesty," Father said gravely. He flicked his hand outward, a gesture to the gentleman behind him, who handed him a small bundle, which he then offered to the queen. "I here present the keys to the valuables Sir Andrew Dudley sent to Skipton, and their inventories."

The sudden and unexpected reminder of those treasures was overwhelming. Memories of that day when they had arrived flashed before my eyes. It was almost beyond belief that only a few weeks later circumstances could be so different.

One of the men at the table stepped forward and took the bundle. The queen then looked directly at me and her expression tightened. Then she said harshly, "Sir Andrew

Dudley and his brother the duke would have turned on each other, just as the Seymour uncles of my late brother did."

There were murmurs of agreement; everyone understood her reference and agreed. I remembered that before Northumberland had come to power, King Edward had been dominated by the two brothers of his mother, Queen Jane Seymour. They had struggled for control, and in the end both had died.

I felt light-headed, but it seemed that I was required to make some remark. The queen's eyes were penetrating. It felt as if she knew everything Sir Andrew and I had spoken about, his ambitions and mine.

A wave of darkness closed in on me. Distantly I heard cries and gasps as my knees buckled and I pitched forward.

When I opened my eyes, I was staring directly into the face of the queen. She was sitting on the floor, cradling my head in her lap. In her eyes I saw genuine concern.

Above us, Mrs Brograve's voice was shrill with anger. "And on the way in here, your soldiers said horrible things to her — just horrible! And she's exhausted after all these days of hard riding to pay her respects to you…"

Dazed, I managed to grasp that she, unbelievably, was upbraiding the queen.

"Quiet, madam!" Father was ordering her. "You do not speak so to the queen!"

"— and you, her own cousin, and her poor mother cold in her grave these six years, who but you should she turn to —"

"Madam!" Father shouted.

But the queen was ignoring them. "She's recovered," she announced. To me, she said, "You fainted. You must be exhausted after your trip."

Seeing that my eyes were open and I was moving, Mrs Brograve fell silent. Father had stepped forward and taken her by the wrist. "Your Grace, please forgive the impertinence of my daughter's attendant."

"Are you able to stand?" the queen asked me.

"Yes," I whispered. She gently helped to lift me into a sitting position, and then up, rising herself, the sea of red damask receding around her. When we were both standing, she gently smoothed out one sleeve of my dress.

Having recovered enough breath to speak, I immediately echoed Father. "Your Grace, I beg you to please forgive Mrs Brograve's outburst."

Mrs Brograve had suddenly understood the extent of her error. Clearly frightened, she had shrunk back against Father. The queen turned her face toward her for barely more than an instant before saying, "She has the look of an honest woman, who said nothing more than the truth. Would to God that all my subjects did so."

Cheers erupted from all the men in the room. When one called out, "God save good Queen Mary!" it was quickly repeated numerous times.

Mrs Brograve rushed forward and threw herself face-down on the floor before the queen. "Begging your forgiveness, Your Highness!" she wailed.

"Get up, good woman. There is nothing to forgive. I thank you for your attendance on my young cousin and for reminding me of my failure to offer the most basic hospitality. It was most un-Christian of me and I will remember to confess it." Her face was almost blank and she spoke in a clipped, matter-of-fact way. She beckoned to an usher. "Take them to the suite of rooms beside my own and see them well attended."

To Father, she said, "My good earl, we will seek your counsel shortly regarding matters in the north."

She turned back to the table, and the usher led us away. As we left, I heard her saying, "Eleanor Brandon was married into the north to establish a Tudor presence there. Northumberland unified himself with the south through marriages and wanted to do the same in the north. Had my brother lived longer, there is no telling the havoc that would have been wreaked. These are the mysterious ways of the Lord."

In a passage outside the hall we were met by a short, black-clad, grey-haired woman about ten years older than the queen, who said her name was Mrs Clarencius. As she led us away, she told us she had been serving the queen for many years, even before the beginning of what she called the 'troubles'. "When her saintly mother Queen Catherine was pushed out by the concubine Boleyn," she explained with disgust.

"The queen likes you," she told me. "Even if she didn't, she would still treat you fairly; her conscience demands it. I was watching from the back when you fainted, and I saw that she sympathised with you. When she was recalled to court after years of banishment, she fainted upon being presented to the king. This is a queen who will never forget the past. She may forgive those who wronged her and her mother — the holy Lord in heaven wants us to forgive those who have harmed us — but she will never forget." She smiled knowingly at me. "Luckily for you, your grandmother was one of the strongest supporters of Queen Catherine, one of the few who dared to let her brother the king see her disapproval. Some even say she died for it, poisoned by the concubine, who feared her influence on King Henry. Others say it was sadness over the whole sorry matter that brought on her illness." She shrugged noncommittally. "Who knows? But the queen remembers her support. It's what's already saved the Duchess of Suffolk and her husband, and will — given time — save Jane."

After passing through a maze of corridors and up a stairway, we arrived at a heavy wooden door. Mrs Clarencius threw it open, and we entered a room luxuriously appointed with colourful tapestries and heavy oak furniture. "Yes, the queen likes you," she repeated. "She wouldn't have put you in here, otherwise. She had it readied for the Marchioness of Exeter, who we've been expecting, but we learned today she will join us later in the week. Do you know her?"

"No." The bed with its embroidered covers and pillows looked almost maddeningly inviting. "I've been away from court for years."

"So has the marchioness." Mrs Clarencius went to each window and opened it, allowing a soft breeze to enter the room. Beside me, an exhausted and subdued Mrs Brograve sank down onto a chair.

Mrs Clarencius eyed her disapprovingly, then continued, "She's another one who suffered because of the concubine's hatred for Queen Catherine. Her husband died because of it, and her son's been locked up in the Tower for years. They're all afraid of him because he has a claim to the throne, older than the Tudors, from the House of York. There are some who would even say he's the rightful king of England." She leaned in and winked at me. "Now, he's got a good chance to become king — by marrying the queen."

This final bit in the torrent of information stood out. I became instantly alert. "The queen will marry?"

"Almost certainly. She wishes to have a child to succeed her. She feels it is God's destiny for her. And it's not too late, God willing. She is thirty-seven, and still has her monthly flow. She has time before she is no longer able." She stopped, clasped her hands together, and looked up at the ceiling. "Even if her flow had stopped, it still wouldn't be too late. Remember Sarah, the wife of Abraham, who gave birth at a time much too late for a woman, because God willed it? Our queen has already shown herself blessed and favoured in her triumph over her enemies, despite great odds. Now, she intends to thank the Lord by bringing England back to the one true faith, and ensuring she leaves a legacy that won't be challenged." Her small brown eyes narrowed, and little lines appeared around her mouth. "And she's not going to leave her throne to that dreadful Elizabeth, daughter of the concubine." She folded her arms decisively. "The only way to make sure of it is by having a child of her own."

Her eyes darted around the room appraisingly. "Well, all seems in order here. You just climb up onto that bed and have a good sleep." To Mrs Brograve, she said, "There's a pallet for you on the side." She smiled at me. "Don't bother coming down for supper; I'll have it sent up for you, if you're awake. Now, let me see about having your things sent up to you. And I'll see if I can pick out a few nice things of the queen's you may be able to use if we let them out a bit." She went out, the wooden door closing behind her with a thud.

For the first time since we'd left the Great Hall, Mrs Brograve spoke. "That's one who likes to hear her herself talk. Full of importance, now her lady's become a queen."

Wearily, I sank down onto the chair beside her. "Can a woman of the queen's age have a child?"

"Great care would have to be taken."

I pulled off my hood, letting my hair flow down on either side of my face. "It's always about having a child. King Edward rushed Jane and me toward marriage to produce one to protect his religion. Now, this queen wants one to protect hers. And both are absolutely sure they must do so to please God." I couldn't help but utter a short, wry laugh.

"Little swan, best not to say such things."

"I wonder what God wants of me, or what the queen wants. Do you think she trusts me? Can a woman like that really trust anyone? I hope she can. For I tell you this: if she doesn't trust me, she'll never allow me to marry and have a child who could take the throne. She thinks she is doing God's work."

"There is kindness in her face. She knows what it is to suffer."

Without understanding how I knew it, I said, "She will be kind and generous and merciful. But in the end, she'll treat me the same way she was treated. She was prevented from marrying and having a child. Others feared the power it would give her."

"Then make her trust you," Mrs Brograve replied, with quiet urgency.

There was a knock on the door. She got up, opened it, and took the few things I'd brought from Skipton. With them was a long robe of green velvet, trimmed with cloth of gold. "A fine robe of the queen's," she said as she offered it to me.

I sank my hands into the rich, soft velvet. "I'm so tired."

"Let me help you to bed."

Once again, I was nearly overcome with fatigue. "Did you hear what that Clarencius creature said about my grandmother being poisoned?"

"Yes."

The story my father had told me, of my mother's belief that her brothers and sons had been poisoned, and that she was being poisoned herself, swirled around in my mind. Abruptly, it lurched into immediate relevance. My grandmother too had still been young enough to have more children when she'd died, perhaps a boy who could have become king. For the Tudor women, bearing children was indeed of great importance.

8

When I opened my eyes, I at first couldn't remember where I was. When I did, I noticed the windows were bright with sunlight, which they hadn't been when I had collapsed into the bed. That had been late afternoon, and it was now morning; I had slept for a very long time.

I leaned up on one elbow. On the far side of the room, a strange woman who looked to be in her mid-twenties was sitting stiffly in a chair, doing nothing. Seeing me stir, she jumped up and hurried over. "Good morning, Lady Margaret," she said deferentially. Her face was pleasant, her expression, though tense, open and without guile. Strands of her fair hair were out of place, and the collar of her dress was a little dishevelled.

"Who are you?" I asked.

There was an edge to my tone, and the tension in her hazel eyes instantly sharpened to fear. She twisted her fingers. "Mrs Newton. I'm here to attend you."

"I don't need you," I said dismissively. "Send for Mrs Brograve."

"Who is that?" She was so frightened she could barely ask the question.

"The woman who arrived with me."

"She's gone."

"Gone?" I sat bolt upright. "What do you mean, gone?"

"She left at dawn." Mrs Newton wrung her hands in agitation.

My first thought was that she had been sent away as a punishment for having dared chastise the queen yesterday. If so, it wasn't fair, and I would have her brought back immediately, even if the decision had been the queen's and not Father's. Whether the queen liked it or not, she was going to understand that not only was I a Tudor also, but I was also the daughter of a great earl with much power in the north. I threw off the cover, which landed at the feet of the cowering woman.

"Send for my father," I ordered.

"The Earl of Cumberland?" she whispered.

"Yes."

"He's gone."

I wheeled around in shock.

"They both left at dawn," she feebly explained. "Mrs Clarencius told me last night to be ready to attend you this morning. She also said you should see her as soon as you were up and dressed."

"I will see the queen," I said, allowing my anger to push away the wave of fear and uncertainty that had washed over me. "Now, help me dress."

Mrs Newton went back to the table and picked up a russet-coloured silk dress. "We sat up late, altering this to fit you," she said, holding it up. "We measured it against the one you had on yesterday. It should fit —"

"Get the green silk I brought with me," I interrupted. The russet colour would favour me, but I would wear nothing but the Tudor green.

Her hands trembled. "But, Lady Margaret, the queen's women all wear black or russet. Other dresses are being prepared for you."

The queen's women? "I am *not* one of the queen's women," I said disdainfully. "I am her cousin. Descended from kings and queens myself!"

Her eyes bulged in terror. She moved toward the door. "I should call Mrs Clarencius —"

"Help me dress right now," I ordered. "And then take me to the queen. I'm going to demand an explanation for all of this!" I turned away so she wouldn't see the tears that were filling my eyes, then cleared my throat. "While I am with the queen, return here and pack my things. I'll be leaving shortly." I felt stronger after my long sleep, capable of riding out alone if need be to return to Skipton. I gestured to the russet silk dress. "And you can leave that here."

Mrs Newton led me through a maze of corridors. We were briefly outside on the battlements, overlooking the army camped around the castle. From this vantage point, its looked even more impressive than it had been yesterday. For the first time since I'd got out of bed, doubts pricked at my angry courage. I'd felt vulnerable yesterday, passing through that army, and then I'd been surrounded by Father and our retinue for protection. Now, even Mrs Brograve wasn't with me.

Back inside we went down another narrow passage; it occurred to me that if need be, I wouldn't even be able to find my way back to the relative security of the room I'd slept in. We went down a flight of stairs. On the floor below, more people were around, talking in low voices and staring as we passed. Their looks all felt suspicious. When we moved into a large room full of arguing and shouting men, my resolve plummeted. Unlike in the hallways, no one even noticed us as we crept through to a door on the other side, with two guards flanking it. By now, my heart had begun to thud, and my temples throbbed. Judging by their attire, the men in the room were important, clearly the leaders of the army outside. Two women gliding through their midst wasn't worth more than a glance for any of them. Some of them must have been present when we'd arrived yesterday, but none now appeared to recognise me.

By the time we reached the guards at the closed door, I was feeling wretchedly insignificant, devoid of any power or authority. Mrs Newton whispered to one of the guards, who in turn whispered to the other. Then one opened the door a fraction, barely enough for the two of us to slip through.

The room we entered was smaller than the outer one and held only a few people. This time, everyone turned and stared at me. There were two men, seated with their backs to each other; it was apparent they disliked each other. Hovering in the background were several women, all dressed in russet silk. One immediately darted over to us and whispered with Mrs Newton, both occasionally glancing at an open door at the far end of the room, which appeared to lead outside.

The sight of several women all dressed in russet served to rally my courage, for to imagine myself blended into such a group was insulting. "I will see my cousin at once," I announced dramatically, and pushed past the whispering women to the open door.

Unexpectedly, it led to a garden, so beautiful I was momentarily taken aback. There were sweet-smelling fruit trees and trickling fountains, and flowerbeds bursting with colour on either side of the walkways. A short way off was the queen with two men beside her, both arguing vigorously. It was clear she was in the middle of mediating some issue. I stopped, not wanting to interrupt an obviously serious matter, but at that moment she saw me.

Behind me, I heard someone emerge through the door, and a heavily breathing russet-clad Mrs Clarencius appeared beside me. She had obviously been alerted by the guards and must have run to reach me. The queen's gaze shifted to her, and something appeared to pass between them. Very gently, Mrs Clarencius placed her hand on my arm. "Your father left you a letter," she said, withdrawing it from her sleeve and offering it. "Come and sit down to read it. I'm sure you'll feel much better afterward."

The queen, seeing the letter offered, immediately looked back at one of the two arguing men, neither of whom had noticed the lapse in her attention. She spoke to them, her voice loud enough for me to catch a few words about confiscated monastic lands.

I grasped the folded letter as Mrs Clarencius led me to a bench beside an ornamental pool. She then retreated and hovered a few feet away as I read it.

Dear Margaret,

The queen has need of my involvement in certain matters at York, which demand my immediate departure. I have no doubt you will be greatly disturbed by my absence when you read this, and angry, and you may feel betrayed — which you have not been. Until this very morning I had intended to tell you I had decided it best for you to remain with the queen, but seeing you still so deeply asleep just now when I arrived in your room, I chose not to wake you.

The queen has most graciously agreed to make a place for you among her women, both here and eventually at her court in London. This course, for which there are numerous reasons, was decided by me before we departed from Skipton. It required much thought on my part, as well as an overcoming of my deep reluctance to be parted from you. But I am convinced this will assist you in ways I cannot, and will have an outcome most beneficial to you, and the unfolding of your life.

Be assured the decision was mine, except for my usual consultation with the stars. Her Majesty does, though, have your best interests at heart. She is especially concerned with any possible marriage for you, and has told me to refrain from discussions of such without her initial involvement. I am sure you see the wisdom of this, especially considering the happenings of the last several months.

My dear daughter, I urge you to take fullest advantage of the position in which you have now been placed. Few indeed have the good fortune to be so close to their sovereign, and the association can benefit you for the rest of your life. It is this only which consoles me on your absence, which I contemplate with a deep sense of loss. Never doubt my great and abiding love for you.

I will see you next in some weeks' time, when I visit London for the queen's coronation. Be well, and be a credit to myself and the queen; always remember the great house from which you and she originate.

Mrs Brograve adds her farewells to mine.

Your loving father,

Henry Cumberland

Sadness and loss settled over me as I finished reading, replacing the lingering anger that had drained away as I'd read. Father had written that he understood I'd feel betrayed, which I did. But I also felt tricked: I'd have refused to move from Skipton Castle had I known his intent. I couldn't remember a time when I'd been away from him for more than a day or two.

Distantly, I could hear the queen still in conversation with her companions. But there were other, more pleasant sounds: birds singing, and branches rustling in the breeze. I continued to look down at the letter as though I hadn't finished reading, to hold at bay the need to talk to Mrs Clarencius, still lurking behind me. It would be futile, I knew, to argue or attempt to leave. Far better for me to pretend not only acceptance of the situation, but satisfaction. Although Father's deviousness was unforgiveable, I grudgingly had to admit that there was wisdom in his decision.

I sat up on the bench and folded the letter, holding it on my knee. Looking up, I saw the queen had finished with the men, who were now gone, and she was coming toward me. Memories of the days of boredom at Brougham surfaced in my mind; the ones ahead were bound to be very different, a prospect I did not find unappealing. I stood and curtsied as she reached me.

"So you will remain with us," she said. She seemed preoccupied by her previous conversation.

"If it pleases Your Majesty."

"Yes. Are you sufficiently rested?"

"I am. The long sleep did me well. Although I wish I'd been able to bid my father farewell."

"Separation from a parent is difficult," she said, as though her own past had broken into her thoughts. "Your father felt it better for you to rest. I agreed and told Mrs Clarencius not to wake you for Mass. Tomorrow morning, we leave for Ipswich, our first stop on our way to London."

"I will be ready."

"Be gentle with Mrs Newton. I selected her for you."

"I'm sure she will be fine."

"Be patient. The good Lord rewards those who learn to be so." She then reached into the sleeve of her dress, withdrawing an object and handing it over to me. Her hands were pale and slender, almost too slight for the numerous rings on her fingers.

It was a small cross of gold, covered with jewels. "A gift of welcome," she said. She didn't smile, her face retaining the same remote look it had had earlier, her low voice neutral. It was impossible to tell how she really felt about me, but the gift seemed a good sign of sincerity, especially with its religious significance.

I thanked her. Without another word, she turned and walked toward the door. I held the cross up, seeing that it was covered with diamonds and rubies.

"A rich gift," Mrs Clarencius said admiringly. "The queen is generous."

"Indeed, she is," I replied, setting the cross within Father's letter, and folding it away.

9

Over the next few days I found that I missed Father terribly, and every night I wept into my pillow, silently, so as not to alarm Mrs Newton, who slept on a pallet in the room with me. Mrs Clarencius said that once we were established in the palaces of London, I was to have two rooms, and perhaps a second attendant, if I found I needed one, and both could sleep in the outer room. But until then, at night I would need to conceal my tears. Mrs Newton became alarmed very easily. She had never aspired to attend so great a lady, as she called me, and was terrified she would prove inadequate. But she was more than competent, willing to attend to trivial matters, and she rode well and travelled with ease, which I saw during the trip from Framlingham Castle to Ipswich. She could also read and write. Her comments at times were astute: early on, she remarked that my new position was 'neither fish nor fowl', observing that although I dressed as one of the queen's women, and conformed to their daily routine, I wasn't one of them, but at the same time, I wasn't treated as an honoured guest, like the nobility who flocked to the queen as we progressed toward London. Together, she and I learned how to negotiate my new and unusual position, and although her timidity annoyed me, I took satisfaction in seeing it diminish as her confidence grew.

It was at Ingatestone Hall that my position became more defined, when the queen's entourage was joined by the Marchioness of Exeter. "She was one of the queen's mother's most devoted supporters," Mrs Clarencius told the women before she arrived, "and she suffered for it. Her husband was of the ancient royal family, a grandson of the Yorkist King Edward." Some of the women glanced at me at the mention of the royal family, but quickly looked away. All had been pleasant and helpful, but also reserved; I wasn't one of them.

Mrs Clarencius continued, "Fifteen years ago, the marquis, with his wife and young son, was imprisoned on suspicion of favouring the old religion, and plotting to seize power to restore it. The charges were meritless, but the king had begun to fear the marquis's strength and royal lineage, even though they had been raised together as cousins." She sniffed contemptuously. "The self-serving Reformers were to blame for arousing his suspicions, and they played upon his resentment of the support the marquis and the marchioness had shown Queen Catherine. The marquis was condemned, stripped of his property, and executed. A year or so later, the marchioness was released, but her son has been kept in the Tower ever since. The Reformers feared he would be a threat to the young king, and held him there even after King Henry died. Now, finally, he will be released, praise God. And his sufferings may soon be well rewarded. There are many who already encourage the queen to choose him as a husband."

One of the women asked if they were the same age. "No," Mrs Clarencius replied. "He's a number of years younger than her — ten, I believe. But for those of royalty, that matters little."

The age difference between myself and Sir Andrew hadn't seemed to matter; our proposed marriage had been for ambition, and I supposed for the queen, it would be the same. Her ambition wouldn't be for the throne, which she'd already achieved, but for lineage, especially to overcome the illegitimacy with which she'd been tarnished. A husband with a clear and undisputed claim to the throne would be exactly what she would seek in the father of her children. The marchioness's son was an excellent candidate, and no doubt his mother's imminent arrival would facilitate it. The marchioness was likely to be formidable. Against great odds, she had succeeded where so many others had failed: she had brought to adulthood a son who could have been crowned as king.

The marchioness, accompanied by a mere two servants, was dressed entirely in black when later that morning she rode up to the front of Ingatestone Hall. The queen, with all of her women, was waiting for her at the front door, and, with a childlike lightness of step, she hurried over to help her dismount, exclaiming, "Welcome! Welcome, dearest marchioness!" For the first time, I heard happiness in the queen's deep voice.

"Most gracious Majesty," said the marchioness, her voice smooth as polished silver. She attempted to kneel, but the queen grasped her and prevented it. Wrapping her arm around her, she led her toward the house. As they passed us, I could see both weeping quietly, the queen's head leaning on the marchioness's shoulder.

"We go first to the chapel, to thank God for not forgetting us," the queen said.

"Oh, yes," said the marchioness, as they entered through the front door. "And let us pray for the soul of your most gracious mother."

Back inside, I told Mrs Newton, "The marchioness is the very image of the 'great lady' you talk about. She's tall; the top of the queen's head barely touches her shoulder. Her clothes are old and out of style, her servants were dressed like paupers, and the nags they rode up on looked ready to collapse. Clearly, she's been kept in near poverty. But even so, she looks refined and elegant. It's the way she carries herself: she sat proudly and gracefully on her horse as she rode up. Her hair is iron-grey, her face worn but beautiful. Despite her age, and all her troubles, she looks noble."

At dinner the marchioness sat on the dais beside the queen, who spoke with her throughout the meal, repeatedly reaching over and patting her hand. At supper, the two dined alone together in the queen's quarters, and remained there afterward.

Resentment pricked at me, for the queen had shown me no such special treatment, and I was a much nearer relative. But the next morning, the marchioness appeared right when the women were assembling for the morning Mass, as though she were merely one of the group, albeit wearing a fine new dress of black silk and an attractive French hood, the style favoured by the queen.

After Mass, she stayed with us in the anteroom as the queen went inside to see the latest of the constant stream of nobility, officials and councillors coming out from London. I had no sooner settled into a chair off to the side, when I saw the marchioness coming toward me. Instinctively, I stood, amused that I did so, for a few months earlier I would not have felt the need to do so. But I was no longer at Brougham or Skipton.

"My dear Lady Margaret," she said as she reached me, extending both her hands. "Or may I take the liberty of calling you cousin, in honour of my dear departed husband and my son?"

Her manner was soft and effortlessly ingratiating, but with an undertone of confidence born of her high status. Yet there wasn't any condescension in her tone; she had approached me as an equal. I suspected that this was how she was with everyone. I replied that nothing would please me more than to be called 'cousin' by her.

She smiled, her blue eyes widening slightly. "Cousin Margaret, then. You are well, I trust? The queen told me your separation from your father was troubling to you."

We sat down. Before I could reply, she said, "But how could it not be? Especially after your narrow escape from your Dudley entanglement."

"I weep every night," I admitted. It was a relief to finally be able to speak honestly with someone.

The marchioness sighed sympathetically. "Dear cousin, life holds all sorts of trials for us. Best to learn to manage them while still young." She reached over and touched my hand. I noticed her skin was hard and calloused, like a servant's. She had been so poor she'd needed to do many things for herself, but it made her admirable.

"I find I miss my mother too, even though she's been dead for so many years," I said. "Never did I think of her so much while I was still at home. But now, it feels as if she's only just died. I don't understand it."

"I knew your mother from when she was born until she left for the north after her marriage. Your grandmother was close to Queen Catherine, as was I, and we all saw each other often. Nearly a lifetime ago, or so it seems. It was a time of happiness and stability, before the changes." She paused. "Before the appearance of the concubine." Her voice sounded brittle. "And the travesties, the utter travesties, that followed."

Her back stiffened, and one of her hands, ringless except for a wedding band, pressed tensely against the black silk of her dress. I waited, not sure how to respond.

Her gaze lowered to the floor, and she pulled a handkerchief from her sleeve. "Forgive me, Cousin Margaret. Speaking of these matters is unfamiliar to me. Long ago, from brutal necessity, I learned the prudence of silence. One never knows who may be listening, and if what you say will be twisted. But now, finally, some things can be talked of without restraint. I said travesties — out of Christian charity, I will not describe it worse. But what followed the onset of the concubine would not have been believed a few years earlier. There was the abandonment of Queen Catherine, her banishment from court, the annulling of her marriage, and the declaration of the bastardy of the good Princess Mary. And the break from the one true religion, which made these things possible." She shook her head sadly. "Only a few years earlier, King Henry had been called 'Defender of the Faith' because of his stand against the Reformers. But they preyed upon his desire for the son that God had not granted to Queen Catherine, and encouraged him to turn away from the truth and declare himself head of the English Church."

Much of this I had heard from my father. "But then Anne Boleyn failed to have a son, also," I said. "The king killed her for it."

"The concubine was executed for adultery," she corrected me, grandly. "Elizabeth, her daughter, was likely the child of her musician, Mark Smeaton." The assertion was shocking, but I thought it best not to say so. The marchioness went on, "We thought matters would return to normal with the third marriage, to Jane Seymour — a gentle, lovely girl I am proud to have worked to advance — and indeed they might have, if she hadn't died giving birth to the son the king had so desperately sought. Her death soured the king and pushed him back into the clutches of the Reformers. Travesty turned to tragedy as the king destroyed any who could threaten the right of the prince to succeed, including my husband and son. Oh, the king suffered, too: two more fiascos of marriages, a third that nearly came to grief as well. But in the end, the Reformers won. They had full control of the prince when the king died, and they've kept it — until now."

She leaned toward me, grasped one of my hands, and whispered urgently, "This queen will right all wrongs! She will lead sweet England back to the golden days before the advent of the concubine! My son will be restored to his rightful place, just as the holy Church will be. The plundering of the monasteries will be righted, and their properties restored. And the Reformers will be removed for good! The queen has already spoken to me of her expectation that England will easily be led back to the one true religion, once those whose greed and opportunism led them to embrace the Reformers are removed."

At the far end of the room, the door the queen had vanished through opened, and three older gentlemen, formally dressed, emerged. On their way out, one of them noticed us and whispered to the others.

"They'll come over now," the marchioness said quietly. "It's the earls of Bedford, Pembroke, and Shrewsbury."

Even before she'd finished speaking, they were coming toward us. Reaching us, each greeted her, and turned inquiring faces toward me.

"The Lady Margaret Clifford," the marchioness offered, adding with authority, "my cousin."

If any of them were surprised, they concealed it admirably and greeted me with deference. Then one said to the marchioness, "We congratulate you, my lady, upon the restoration of your estates. And, the imminent creation of your son, earl of Devon."

"Praise God," she replied, bowing her head. "My son will be happy to receive you in London." As the men left, she said to me, "Six months ago they all would have walked right past me." She smiled. "You'll like my son. He was named Edward, after his great-grandfather, King Edward, just as our last little king — poor misguided child — was. But I have always called him Ned. You must do the same: Cousin Ned."

Mrs Clarencius came up to us. "The Lady Elizabeth has just arrived in London," she announced heavily. "She was escorted in by two thousand men on horseback, all wearing green and white livery. The queen has ordered her to ride out and join us as we approach London. I suppose it was inevitable that she would come at some point."

"Oh!" said the marchioness, with disdain. "Well, we can't expect things to be perfect, can we? And it's a testament to the goodness of the queen that she holds no grudge from the past. Pray God to send me the same capacity for forgiveness. But I'll never forget the shame of my having to carry Elizabeth at her christening. King Henry was punishing me for my support of Queen Catherine." Her smooth and elegant manner cracked just enough for her to wrinkle her nose.

Her anger and resentment over her treatment were still strong, twenty years later. I wondered if it would be the same for the queen, and how she would receive her half-sister.

When they met on the Colchester Road outside London, Lady Elizabeth knelt in homage before the queen, who immediately raised and embraced her, and they kissed each other's cheeks.

"We'll see," murmured the marchioness sceptically, beside me. "She's wearing the plain clothes of a Reformer."

The queen then led Elizabeth toward us. To my surprise, she brought her to me first. "Lady Margaret Clifford, our cousin," she said. Lady Elizabeth and I exchanged kisses. She was nearly as tall as me, well-shaped and clear-skinned, with dark grey eyes and red-gold hair that was abundant and wavy like mine.

105

Our eyes met briefly, long enough for me to see the wariness and shrewdness in hers. She was four years older than me, and so, like me, much younger than the queen. As she stood with her half-sister, holding her hand, the age difference was obvious. Elizabeth looked healthier and livelier, despite her rather simple black and white attire. Beside her, the queen, in her sumptuous gown, looked old and garish, the colourful velvet and sparkling jewels a sad attempt to compensate for her lost youth.

The queen then presented Elizabeth to the marchioness, who responded as though she was delighted by her arrival. "May I take the liberty of calling you cousin?" I heard the marchioness asking, echoing what she had said to me a few days earlier.

The queen's women and the Lady Elizabeth's companions clustered around them, the russet and green of the different liveries blending together. But the many female voices in conversation sounded stilted and forced beneath the veneer of joyful spontaneity.

That night, as Mrs Newton helped me to prepare for bed, I told her how the queen had introduced Elizabeth to me before the marchioness. "I hadn't expected it. She favours the marchioness and appears barely aware of my existence."

"The women all talk of how the queen has no guile. What she does shows what she thinks. She must have wanted the Lady Elizabeth to see you are important."

"Why?"

She looked at me in surprise. "To show her there's another claim to the throne beside hers."

"She is using me as a threat?"

Mrs Newton grimaced but nodded her head.

"Then she herself must see me as a threat too."

She lifted a hand helplessly. "You're young. You shouldn't have any trouble having a child. And no one's ever said your parents weren't properly married." She hesitated. "There's talk among the women. The queen's been heard saying your cousin Jane's father and mother weren't rightly married."

Sir Andrew had spoken to me of it also, that day at Brougham while we were hunting. He'd told me it was a way of removing Jane from the succession, as well as her sisters and Mary and Elizabeth.

"The queen says it may be a way of saving Jane's life, and keeping her out of any more trouble," Mrs Newton said.

For Sir Andrew, it had been a way of moving me closer to the throne. If he had seen it that way, there would be others who would also.

"Don't object or show dissatisfaction if the queen doesn't make much of you," Mrs Newton advised. "Stay in the background with the other women. I saw how she looked today, standing beside her sister — smaller, older, used up by the past. The Lady Elizabeth is feeling strong now. The queen's victory is hers, too — the people won't let the old king's succession be changed. But that's for now. Who knows what may happen?"

I remembered that Mrs Brograve had told me to make the queen trust me. If I couldn't gain her friendship, at least I might be able to avoid her enmity.

10

Quietly and without objection, I accepted my place as merely another of the queen's women for our entry into London, dressed like all the others in the usual russet. The queen's attire was magnificent: she wore a dark blue velvet and satin gown trimmed with gold, many necklaces of gold and pearls, and a French hood studded with jewels. The white horse that had been chosen for her was small, so that the rider might appear less diminutive. Behind her rode the Lady Elizabeth, dressed in white satin, with no jewels or other ornaments: as the marchioness had said yesterday, she wore the dress of a Reformer. She sat her horse well, tall and straight in the saddle, her red-gold hair flowing down over her shoulders from beneath her gable hood. After her came the marchioness, dignified in black velvet, but with necklaces of silver and pearls, and the same gems at the edges of her French hood.

Other finely dressed noblewomen followed, and then the combined women of the queen and Lady Elizabeth, myself among them. Ahead of the queen rode the Earl of Arundel with the Sword of State, and before him were more than a hundred gentlewomen of various distinction, and several hundred gentlemen in velvet coats. Behind us came at least a thousand horsemen, the queen's guard, in uniforms of green and white, red and white, and blue and white. Trailing after them, stretching far back and out of sight, were thousands more of the queen's supporters.

Cheering crowds flocked to the road as our colourful procession wound its way toward the city. The looming stone portal at Aldgate was hung with colourful streamers, and on top of it a platform had been placed, full of children singing songs of welcome for the queen. At the gate, the queen was greeted by the mayor and other city officials, and all of her guard was dismissed. Inside, the city streets were crammed with citizens, cheering and waving banners, and streamers hung from the windows of the tightly packed houses we rode past.

The narrow streets gave way to the Tower, the royal apartments of which would be our residence until King Edward was buried. It was tradition, Mrs Clarencius had explained to the women, some of whom had looked startled upon learning we would stay there. "Only part of the Tower is used as a prison," she had said. "It's a palace, and a fortress, one of the safest places in the city." As it appeared before us, the large stone walls had an unexpected beauty. Spread out on the banks of the Thames river, it also felt airier and more open than the densely packed streets we'd just passed through.

Memories of my last visit to the city the year after King Henry had died stirred within me. I remembered the river, and the novelty of travelling on it between the various palaces. My mother had lived in Suffolk Palace as a child, and one day we'd taken a boat close to London Bridge to see it. It had been built by my grandfather, the Duke of Suffolk. When we'd landed, we'd passed through orchards and gardens so vast it had felt as if we'd left the city. Then we'd explored a three-storey mansion with towers, cupolas and many wings, larger than either of our castles. It had been unoccupied for years. Caretakers had let us inside, and Mother had led us to a remote third-floor room overlooking the river. Father had gently tried to dissuade her, but she had been adamant. "This was your uncle's room," she'd said as she'd led me in by the hand. "He wasn't much older than you are now when he died."

Everything had been covered with dust, but even so it was clear that this was a room fit for a prince. I barely noticed the richness of the wall hangings and the intricately carved oak furniture, and focused instead on the wondrous toys. Leaning against a wall were hoops of all sizes, some with bells attached and sticks to push them with, and a large wooden barrel, standing upright, the type I had liked to roll about. Other sticks piled on the floor had ribbons attached to them. There was a hobby horse, the colourfully painted head perched on the end of a pole. On the tables were little balls, dishes of marbles, dice, little wooden tops and spinning instruments I'd never seen before, a pot of winks, masks, dolls of all shapes and sizes, little stone animals and clay pipes for soap bubbles. In the centre of the room, dangling from the ceiling and away from any furniture, was a swing. I ran over to try it, but Father stopped me. Mother stood at the table, staring at the toys and remembering.

There were other tables, piled with books and objects familiar to me from my own education. Two other rooms led off the main one, one for the servants to sleep in, the other, surprisingly, a kitchen. I asked my mother why it was there.

"All his food was prepared here," she answered in a strange voice.

I then asked why he didn't eat downstairs with everyone else. She started to say something but stopped. Then she said, "He didn't leave these rooms very much. It wasn't safe for him."

She seemed to be about to say more, but Father stepped forward and took her arm. "Eleanor, leave it be," he said. "The past cannot be undone."

She picked up one of the dolls from the table and held it silently, and then abruptly dropped it. She then allowed Father to lead us from the room. Outside, passing through the

110

gardens again as we returned to the river, she suddenly looked back at the mansion and said fiercely, "I will have what is mine again." I thought she meant that we would come back and live there, and perhaps she did. But by the end of that year, she was dead.

Trumpets blared, jolting my thoughts back to the present, and there were cheers as the queen was greeted at the Tower. But what Father had told me at Skipton of the deaths of my mother and brothers, and the little uncle I'd just been thinking of, weighed heavily on my mind. They'd been poisoned to clear the way for someone else to inherit the sonless King Henry's throne. So much that I had not understood about our visit to Suffolk Palace that day was now perfectly clear. The Earl of Lincoln had passed his short life sheltered in luxurious rooms with the finest toys. His life had been at stake, and when his main protector, my grandmother, had died, he had barely outlived her. The lioness had protected her royal cub only as long as she'd been able to protect herself.

Ahead of me, I saw the queen, the Lady Elizabeth, and the marchioness. There were other lionesses now who would seek to have cubs, to be a future king. They would struggle to protect them, and they wouldn't want competition. Eagles usually hatched only one offspring, and when at times there were two, the stronger would eventually kill the weaker. Ahead of me, the queen and Lady Elizabeth were now almost side by side, with the marchioness hovering directly behind them. My inconspicuous placement among the women now felt fortunate, and I thought I'd been wise to leave my golden eagle brooch safely concealed at Skipton.

Inside the Tower walls was a wide-open space, where everyone dismounted, a multitude of grooms rushing about, leading the horses away. At the far end was a little church, before which were a number of finely dressed men and women, all of whom knelt as the queen approached. Most conspicuous was a tall man with golden hair, whose striking good looks became increasingly apparent as we drew closer. The queen actually ran the final distance to reach the kneeling group, looking like a scampering child dressed up in her mother's finery. Reaching them, she burst into tears and kissed each one as she raised them. The handsome man stood taller than all of them, and the queen in particular seemed dwarfed by him, her head barely reaching his chest. Close up, I could see his eyes were blue, his complexion fair and smooth, set off by the impeccable black satin he wore.

This was the man whose mother had already decided I would call Cousin Ned. "Most gracious Majesty," he said in a smooth and melodious voice, as he smiled down at Mary.

The queen quickly turned around, and I saw that her expression was uncertain but oddly happy. Her hands came together, her fingers fluttering, and for an instant I thought she might giggle. But then she said imperiously, her voice even deeper than usual, "May I present to all of you this gentleman, Edward Courtenay, a descendant of kings. Soon he will become Earl of Devon, the first of many wrongs to be righted."

Everyone in the crowd applauded. The marchioness gave a little gasp, and her hands flew to her face. "Praise God for your goodness to my son!" she exclaimed as he stepped forward and bowed. Again, the crowd applauded, a little more strenuously than seemed appropriate, as though they were acknowledging their future king. Beside the marchioness, the Lady Elizabeth turned and looked at the open space before the church. Others must have noticed her shift in attention also, because behind me someone whispered, "It's where her mother was executed."

"Will all wrongs be righted?" someone else replied quietly.

After the ceremony the great crowd began to disperse, some leaving the Tower, while those of us in the queen's household made our way toward the royal apartments. With the formalities over, I found myself walking beside two of the queen's gentleman. One of them told the other, "Jane's being kept in that house, between the lieutenant's lodging and the Beauchamp Tower." I turned and looked as he pointed behind us to a smaller building nestled between a modern timber-faced house and a tall, looming tower with small windows. "But all the Dudley men are in the Beauchamp Tower, close to where they put the block out for chopping off heads!" The man laughed cruelly.

"Better there than in the tower where those little princes were killed," his companion replied. "Where was that?"

"The Garden Tower." He pointed to the right, by the gate we had entered through. "Down there."

Where the little princes were killed? I had no idea what he was talking about.

The second gentleman said, "They say their ghosts still walk here some nights. Two little boys together, walking toward the White Tower. And then they just fade into the wall — the same way they disappeared."

"And that's how the Tudors got the throne." The remark was made with utter nonchalance, as if this was something everyone knew. Everyone, it seemed, but me.

The apartments for the queen's gentlewomen were cramped and uncomfortable, but Mrs Clarencius assured us we would only be there for two weeks at most, before moving to Richmond Palace. Mrs Newton and I had to share a room with two other women and their attendants. Mrs Newton was plainly disgusted by the plan, and felt it was insulting to me, but I couldn't have cared less. Since overhearing the remarks about the murder of the princes, I'd been able to think of little else; even the display of the Crown Jewels in the White Tower had barely held my attention. I wanted to ask the marchioness about it, since, given her age and position, she was the person most likely to know if there were any truth to the tale. But the marchioness was understandably unavailable, having been reunited with her son. I therefore decided to ask Mrs Clarencius instead.

She blinked several times and looked surprised. "My dear Lady Margaret," she replied, "that story is known by everyone in England."

"My father sheltered me from much, especially after my mother died."

She recited what she knew. "King Edward the Fourth — your great-great-grandfather, and the last Yorkist king — had two young sons, as well as many daughters, including the one who became your great-grandmother. They were both still boys when their father died, and the elder was proclaimed king. Shortly afterward, they were placed here in the Tower for safekeeping. A little while later, their uncle Richard gave out that they were illegitimate and proclaimed himself king. No one ever saw those poor boys again, not even after Henry Tudor — your great-grandfather — claimed the throne and killed King Richard in battle. But by then, everyone just assumed they were dead, murdered by King Richard."

She inhaled deeply and smiled, looking very pleased with her command of my family's history. But then she noticed the revulsion on my face. It was nearly impossible to believe that innocent children could have been murdered in pursuit of the throne. But my family history, it seemed, was replete with instances of this. "I spring from a violent people, it would appear," I said feebly.

"That was all long ago," Mrs Newton said angrily, pushing herself between Mrs Clarencius and myself; she had been nearby and had heard the story. To Mrs Clarencius, she said reproachfully, "Why are you troubling her with such nonsense on such a wonderful day?"

Mrs Clarencius became defensive. "Well, she asked me, didn't she?"

When she was gone, I asked Mrs Newton, "You have heard that tale?"

She looked distressed but answered honestly. "Yes. It is well known, my lady."

I wanted to tell her of the deaths of my brothers and uncles, and my dark thoughts about how a family could be doomed to repeat its past. Instead, I asked if she'd heard of the ghostly apparitions. Unsurprisingly, she had, and they made her shudder.

That night, after the banquets and festivities had concluded with a grand musical display, we had just retired to our communal bedroom when I received a message that the queen wished to see me. The other women, who had been chattering among themselves, stopped and stared. Fear soared within me, but I concealed it and smiled serenely as I sailed out of the room. Behind me, I heard Mrs Newton say, "She's her cousin, isn't she? They probably have some family matter to discuss."

I became calm on the way, telling myself there was no need for concern, for I'd done nothing I could be reproached for.

The queen's room was dim, lit by several candles on a table. She was sitting upright in a wooden armchair, wearing a plain brown robe without ornamentation, all of her jewellery removed. Her rich red hair, severely parted in the centre, was loose and being brushed by Mrs Clarencius, the only one of her women present. Spread out, her hair looked fuller, although still without waves or curls.

The queen gestured for me to sit on a footstool beside her. I did, for the first time finding myself in a position in which I had to look up to her. She was clearly tired after the day's activities, but not as much as I would have expected. There was a vibrant look to her blue eyes I hadn't seen before, and she looked younger.

Mrs Clarencius ran the brush down her long hair one final time. It was silver-backed, with jewels, and I remembered a similar one among the rich gifts Sir Andrew had sent me at Skipton. Ruthlessly, I pushed the thought of it away.

Mrs Clarencius retreated to the other side of the room, vanishing into the shadows.

"Lady Margaret," said the queen, "I have been remiss in my attention to you." Despite her informal appearance, her voice was as deep as ever and seemed louder, perhaps because I was rarely so near her. "Please forgive me."

"Your Majesty has had much to attend to."

"I forget you have been placed here away from family and friends. This is particularly wrong, since God has shown such favour to me of late. I will do better."

"You are kind, Your Grace."

"You have today asked questions about our mutual ancestors." The shift in subject was jarring, but there was no change in her tone or demeanour. "About my grandmother's, who was your great-grandmother's, brothers. The king and prince who vanished here in the Tower after being declared illegitimate when King Richard seized the throne. What prompted your questions?"

"Gentlemen commented on it on our way inside today."

"Which ones?"

If I searched my memory, I might have been able to describe them. But I sensed that I should say as little as possible, without lying. "I don't know," I replied. "They were beside me, and I only glimpsed them sideways after the remark drew my attention. They were wearing your livery, and all the gentlemen look much the same to me in it."

She was silent, her eyes fixed on me. Then she said, "No one knows who killed them." I felt my entire body relax; she wasn't suspicious of me. She went on, "Some people believe it was my grandfather, Henry Tudor, but that couldn't be true. God favoured Henry Tudor in bringing him victory over King Richard, and God would not have done that for a murderer of children. If God is with you, none can be against you."

Bitterness seized me. "My mother died six years ago, and my brothers and uncles died as children. It is said they were poisoned. Was God not with them?"

"The ways of God are mysterious," the queen answered quickly, her tone empathetic, but with traces of her own bitterness. "He allowed my mother to suffer, and me. But he protected me from my enemies, and now look at where he has brought me. I hold the position my mother desired for me above all else."

I folded my hands. "I'd thought my mother died of illness. It was hard for me to believe the tales my father told me. I was hoping they weren't true. But I see now that they are, and there is no use pretending otherwise. My mother was poisoned, and my brothers and uncles before her."

"And the little princes of Scotland," the queen added flatly. "The brothers of the Scottish queen."

My grandfather had been suspected of those murders, in retaliation for those of my brothers. The queen clearly knew this, and she wanted me to know she knew it. "Yes," I said in acknowledgement. "I was told that too."

She gave a short sigh, and her head tilted slightly, enough for the candlelight to play differently on her face, bringing out her nearly invisible eyebrows and better defining her features. "I have survived two poisoning attempts, which took place during the years of the concubine. Both times an inertia came over me, similar to the one that killed your mother, I hear. Certainly, it was the same poison. But I quickly found a good doctor." She paused. "Some time after your mother died, your father was stricken with a similar illness. He lay as though dead."

I gasped. "He said nothing of that to me! And I don't remember it."

She tilted her head again. The light shifted, and her face seemed to soften. "It was unlikely he or anyone in attendance wished to burden you. It is believed he ate or drank something tainted that had been intended for your mother, but had gone unused. Upon recovering, it is said that he was mad with fear that you would be harmed the same way."

"How did you come to know of this?" I asked, still scarcely believing it.

"My mother, God rest her soul, taught me that my life depended on knowledge of what transpired around the throne. It was a lesson well learned. Her friends became mine, and I continued to cultivate others throughout the kingdom. This is how I knew my brother was being influenced into changing the succession, and how I was able to prepare for it in advance."

Apparently, this was the way of it among the powerful: I remembered Sir Andrew's ability to convey messages quickly from London to Skipton. In a small voice, I said, "My father never spoke of this. Only recently did he tell me of the other matters."

The queen shifted in her chair. "Your Father is wise. I am sure he chose to tell you following the appearance of Sir Andrew Dudley in your life. He was trying to show you the need for caution, that the world was a dangerous place, where people would stop at nothing to take the throne." She leaned toward me, her face tightening angrily. "Let me tell you something of the Dudleys. What they really wanted was revenge. The father of the duke was executed by my father, for crimes committed during my grandfather's reign. They have a way about them, those Dudleys, with their silver tongues and their charm, and Edmund Dudley had weaselled himself into a position of confidence. Through underhand measures, he drained the nobility of wealth, bringing some to the king and a fortune to himself. It was a wrong my father righted: Dudley was convicted of treason and executed. My father treated his widow and sons with the greatest generosity, advancing them and never holding their father's treachery against them. But they harboured a grudge all these years and sought revenge by aiming to take the throne from the Tudors."

Her little hands were grasping the elaborately carved wooden arms of her chair. "We know from more than one report that the duke intended to have his son Guildford crowned king. Among the Crown Jewels there is a new coronet, of gold and diamonds, made for a man. Who else could that have been for but a new king? We know that poor Lady Jane understood enough to refuse the throne the first time she was asked to take it, but how long could she have held out against them?

She has already said she believes they intended to poison her once that was accomplished. Perhaps she is mistaken, for my reports indicate that they wanted a child. But how long would Lady Jane have survived following the birth of a Dudley heir to the kingdom?" Her hands relaxed and she leaned back in her chair, still eyeing me intently. I remained silent, fearful of saying the wrong thing. I lowered my eyes and bowed my head.

More quietly, she went on, "Lady Margaret, how long would you have survived your marriage to Andrew Dudley? Especially if the question of Jane's legitimacy came into play, and you'd had a child before her? These brothers would have turned on each other. Your life would have been in danger. Be grateful for the intervention of God."

The unexpected touch of her hand on the side of my face caused me to look up at her. She wasn't smiling, but there was sincerity in her blue eyes.

"I have been but the instrument of God in saving you from a terrible fate," she said. "He has placed you under my protection, and I will not fail him. Be assured that you are secure here with me. And now, I will keep you from your rest no longer."

Mrs Clarencius emerged from the shadows and escorted me to the door. As the guards closed it behind me, I heard the queen say something to her about Edward Courtenay. This morning he had seemed the perfect picture of male beauty and grace. The reason for the new look of youth about the queen was clear.

One of the guards pointed out the corridor leading back to the women's rooms. It was dark, lit by occasional flickering tapers. I welcomed the moment of solitude, for I needed to compose myself before rejoining my companions. They would no doubt scrutinise my demeanour for clues as to what had transpired with the queen.

The story of the Dudleys' motive for revenge on the Tudors had a ring of truth to it, but the queen was too willing to dismiss the powerful influence of King Edward's religious convictions. Even with my limited knowledge of court politics, it was easy to see that without it the Dudleys would never have come to power. So strong was the queen's belief in her own religious rightness that she failed to see that her brother had been equally devout. But what had been clear to her was that my having a child before Jane would have threatened Guildford and the duke. And surely, for all her sincerity, she was thinking the same would be true for herself if I had a son before she did.

I had reached the door to my room, but I was so agitated that the thought of entering it was impossible, so I continued down the corridor. I reached a station of several guards and asked if there was a place I could take some air. They whispered together, then the one in charge told two of them to go with me.

The took me to a doorway that led to an upper walkway on one of the inner tower walls. They lingered by the door, while I went out into the moonlit summer night. The air was cool and carried the scent of the river.

I half leaned, half sat against a low stone wall and breathed deeply. The grounds of the Tower spread out before me; across the open space I saw the Beauchamp Tower and beside it the house that Jane was in. I wondered at the fate that had drawn us all together in one place: the queen, Jane, Sir Andrew and his family, the Lady Elizabeth, and the marchioness and her son. It seemed we were all participants in some strange masque, our true identities hidden, on display for an audience who cared little what the outcome would be.

In the shadows below me, something shifted. Very briefly, two small, ghostly shapes seemed to form and then dissolve against the wall. Startled, I stepped toward the opposite low wall to see better, but there was nothing but the moonlight. Back by the door, the guards appeared not to have noticed a thing. I turned and went back inside, ready to resume my place in the masque.

11

It was two months before I saw Father again, at the queen's coronation. I'd received letters from him but hadn't written back, still angry about his betrayal and abandonment of me at Framlingham. It mattered little that I had very quickly understood the wisdom of his decision; it was the way he had done it that I found so insulting. He didn't deserve to know that I missed him and my homes so terribly that there'd been nights when I'd been on the verge of simply returning by myself. I wasn't sure if what had kept me at court was my fear of the queen's anger if I left without her permission, or my determination not to let him see how much the separation had affected me.

He arrived in London the day before the coronation, but didn't visit me because of my involvement with the endless festivities associated with the queen's procession though the city. The next day I first caught sight of him in the crowd at Westminster Abbey, straining to find me among the queen's women. When he finally approached me in the chaos preceding the banquet in the Great Hall of Whitehall Palace, I couldn't maintain my pretence of indifference and joyfully threw my arms about his neck. He was dressed in finery — a dark grey damask doublet and a wide-shouldered black box coat, trimmed with fur — but his scent was a relief from the ever-present perfumes of the courtiers. It reminded me of the north, of wide-open fields with galloping horses and soaring hawks against an endless blue sky. I longed for the familiar stone walls and muddy courtyards of Brougham and the rolling landscape surrounding Skipton.

"A touching reunion," said a smooth female voice behind me; it was the marchioness. She wore her usual black velvet but with many jewels. Over the past few weeks, their quantity had steadily increased, gifts not only from the queen but also from others at court, a pointed demonstration of the favour she continued to enjoy. Various earls, viscounts, barons and other courtiers were finding their way to her, understanding she had the ear of the queen.

Beside her was her son — Cousin Ned, as she'd asked me to call him — resplendent in white and gold velvet. Royal favour had been showered on him, and he was now Earl of Devon, with many estates and a luxurious London house.

Father and the marchioness greeted each other familiarly — they had known each other in the years of King Henry, before the downfall of the marchioness's husband — and she then presented Cousin Ned to Father.

He stood as tall as Father, but despite the easy grace of his movements, his posture was stiff, and upon introduction to Father, it grew stiffer, as though he felt threatened. His large blue eyes narrowed slightly, and his handsome head tilted upward. He said something in Latin to Father. Although I knew Latin, his was much better than mine, the result of hours of study and application during his years in the Tower, and I couldn't grasp the meaning. But even so, the name of the Duke of Northumberland, in English, had been clear.

The duke was dead. Very quickly he had been tried, with several others, including Sir Andrew, and all had been found guilty of treason. The duke alone had been executed, despite converting to the old religion and attending Mass in a desperate attempt to gain a pardon from the queen. But she had remained implacable, and he had gone to the headsman's block on Tower Hill, in front of ten thousand onlookers. The man I had never seen, but who had impacted my life so deeply, was now permanently removed from it. The consequences of his actions, though, remained unresolved: Jane and the other members of the Dudley family were still to be tried, and Sir Andrew remained in the Tower, condemned. It seemed likely that all would be pardoned, and eventually released, since the queen was eager to move on from the disturbances. Hopefully my involvement with Sir Andrew would also be left in the past, and she would forget whatever fears she still harboured regarding me and my ability to produce a child who could threaten her throne.

Those fears, I suspected, would not be completely allayed until she had a child of her own, preferably a boy. One of the most discussed topics among the queen's women, and the entire court, was the expectation that she would marry as soon as possible, and the most eligible candidate was clearly the new Earl of Devon: Cousin Ned.

His use of Latin when speaking to Father had been unsurprising. Over the past few weeks at court, he had shown his command of languages — not only Latin and Greek, but also French, Spanish and Italian — with the pride of a colourful bird displaying its plumage. But what was unusual was his mention of the recently executed duke.

Father replied at once, in perfect Latin, and Cousin Ned seemed surprised. Often, those he used it with quickly admitted their lack of understanding, after which he would repeat himself in English, with just a touch of condescension. But then he would smile languidly, looking ever so handsome, and his mysterious charm would erase any affront the person might have felt.

This time, he frowned slightly and said something in a language I didn't understand. Father instantly answered in the same language, and this time it was he who included a reference to the duke.

Cousin Ned then said flatly, "Any books for my library are welcome."

"Then I will be most pleased to send you volumes that will enhance it," Father replied.

Genuine pleasure crossed Cousin Ned's face. "Welcome to court, my Lord of Cumberland," he said. Abruptly, he turned to three gentleman of the court who had waited deferentially behind him and rushed away with them.

"Ned!" called his mother, hurrying after him.

"He is much sought-after," I said in a low voice to Father. "It's believed the queen will marry him. What did he say about the Duke of Northumberland?"

A look of amusement crossed Father's face. "He said the queen gave him much of his property and he would sell it to me cheap, if I wanted it. When he saw my Latin was as good as his, he switched to Greek. I answered in Greek that I wanted nothing of Northumberland's, except perhaps if there were ancient volumes of wisdom, but I was sure that if there were, he, being so erudite, would be keeping them."

"At least it wasn't about our entanglement with the Dudleys," I said with relief. "No one here speaks to me of it, although I know some of them think about it, especially the queen's councillors. Not Cousin Ned, though." Father's eyebrows drew together, curiously. I explained, "It's what his mother asked me to call him. They call me Cousin Margaret."

"The marchioness is shrewd. It emphasises their ties to the royal family."

"She is ambitious for her son."

"He is favoured by others beside the queen?"

"Bishop Gardiner, especially. The marchioness told me that, because of his being of the old religion, the bishop had been in the Tower at the same time as Cousin Ned. They'd been allowed to visit each other occasionally and became friends. The queen has appointed him Chancellor. I'm sure you noticed today that he was the one to crown her."

Father's forehead wrinkled pensively. Many more people had come into the Great Hall now, and it was harder to hear each other, so we pulled back toward one of the many window bays. "Have you spent time with the young earl?" he asked.

"Some, with his mother. He's a little strange, but he has an attractive way about him that many respond to. Although the queen hasn't seen him privately, she has showered him with gifts. She also appointed a gentleman to teach him to ride, and how to handle a sword — all the things he never learned in the Tower. Just this past week I accompanied the marchioness to the palace tennis courts to watch him being taught the game, which all the young noblemen are playing now. Most of the queen's women believe these are signs she is preparing him to be king." I hesitated, not wanting to spoil the happiness we were both feeling at our reunion. "The queen has also appointed another gentleman to teach him the ways of the court. He is fortunate: I've had to learn them on my own." Our eyes met, but I quickly looked away: I didn't want to reproach him at the moment. "The marchioness has helped me to find my way here."

There was a commotion at a nearby door, and the Lady Elizabeth entered, dressed in a gown of white and silver, and covered in jewels. The small gold coronet showing her position as heiress presumptive that she'd worn in the procession and ceremony had been removed, but prominently displayed on a heavy chain of gold was a spectacularly jewelled golden cross.

"She's converted to the old religion," I told Father. "She no longer wears the clothes of a Reformer. The new elaborate ones suit her better. She dresses with style and doesn't appear unhappy about discarding her simple Reformer attire. But I'm not sure she feels the same about her new religion."

"The Reformers believe her a legitimate child of the old king, and the queen, illegitimate," Father told me. "I'm surprised she converted."

"The queen made it clear her favour depended on it. At first, Lady Elizabeth declined to attend Mass, but now she comes to both morning and evening services each day. The queen at first showed she would be tolerant of the Reformers, but grows less so every day, according to the marchioness."

"You don't refer to the princess as 'Cousin Elizabeth'?" Father asked with humour.

I let out a small laugh. "Oh, no. We seldom speak, but when we do, we address each other formally. She is pleasant and polite, but very guarded. I feel she may rather like me, but she behaves the same with everyone."

The crowds parted for Lady Elizabeth to reach the dais, followed by her attendants. As she swept by, she turned and looked directly at us, nodding her head in greeting. I smiled in acknowledgement, and Father bowed slightly.

"She knew exactly where we were in this crowd," he said as she passed. "I'm sure she knows exactly who else is here, and where they are." He looked at me meaningfully. "And that, my daughter, is how one not only survives at court, but succeeds —" he glanced sideways, indicating that I should look in that direction — "even without powerful friends, like the Bishop of Winchester." I looked and saw Cousin Edward in conversation with the bishop; the aged, heavy man had his arm protectively around his shoulder and was speaking into his ear. Father then said in a voice so soft I could barely hear it, "Gardiner crowning the queen is a public message from her. Traditionally, this has always been done by the Archbishop of Canterbury. But he is a Reformer."

"He's in the Tower now," I said. "With the other Reformer clergy who refused the queen's order to stop preaching. The marchioness says the queen believes it's only a matter of time until everyone returns to the old religion. She feels that without the support of those who professed it for political reasons, it will die out."

"That remains to be seen," Father replied doubtfully.

An usher approached and asked to seat us. We separated, Father shown to a place of honour close by the queen with the other earls, and me farther back with the queen's women.

There were plays, music, and various other entertainments during and after the sumptuous banquet, all of which lasted until well after midnight. I then briefly said goodnight to Father. As a relation of the queen he'd been given rooms at the palace for his stay, and I would be able to see him in the morning. The queen had held up admirably throughout the evening, eating heartily of the various dishes, enjoying the comedies, and repeatedly calling for various lords to visit her in the centre of the dais. But by the end she had looked exhausted, and Mrs Clarencius told us she would stay in her room the next day, resting.

Mrs Newton had attended the banquet also, seated near the rear of the hall. "Who was the man sitting beside your father? They were in conversation all evening," she said when we'd returned to our rooms.

"The Earl of Shrewsbury. He's another powerful lord of the north."

"Has he a marriageable son?"

She was in the outer of my two rooms, I in the inner one. As promised, at Whitehall and the other palaces I'd been given a two-room suite, one of the few signs I had some status at court. Whitehall was the largest and most comfortable of all the palaces we'd stayed at since leaving the Tower. My rooms were wood-panelled with ceramic stoves and had oriel windows, typical throughout the huge palace.

I went into the front room. "Why do you ask?"

"I saw them both look toward you from time to time, as if they spoke of you."

"He doesn't," I said. "Besides, it's clear the queen will decide who I marry. Given that my proposed marriage was the cause of the difficulty we have recently emerged from, I'd be surprised if Father would initiate discussion of it. We must wait for the queen to do so. And she has many others to decide as well — her own, the Lady Elizabeth's. And the Earl of Devon's. Although it's likely that is who she will marry herself."

Mrs Newton quickly looked away from me, as though she knew more than she wished to say.

"Have you heard something else?" I asked. "You can tell me, without concern."

"There's talk among the servants that the queen no longer favours him. It's said she now wants to marry someone from abroad."

I considered this startling announcement in silence. It would be a devastating blow for the marchioness, to say nothing of Cousin Ned. Certainly, there would be many who would continue to try to bring that marriage about, powerful figures at court, like Bishop Gardiner. Suddenly I was uncomfortable with the discussion. "Tell me of your own husband," I said, changing the subject. "You've never mentioned him in all this time."

"He's dead. I'm a widow."

"But you're so young!"

"I don't mind it," she said easily. "We weren't married all that long, so I can't say I miss him. My parents had picked him out for me, and before I was married, I had to do what they wanted. But now that I'm a widow, I can do what I want. He left me some money. I'm not eager to get married again anytime soon." She was sensitive to my shifting moods, and she must have noticed that I looked surprised. "It's not like it is for you," she said. "No one cares if I have children or not. There's nothing 'royal' or 'noble' about me to pass on."

All at once, a great tiredness overcame me. The red velvet dress that had so pleased me when I'd first put it on now felt much too heavy, and I longed to be rid of it. "Help me out of this, will you?" I asked, running a hand over my face. She came to help me. "Perhaps it would be best if you didn't tell anyone else what you've heard about the queen's wedding plans. Best for us to keep out of it." I smiled gently at her, hiding that I suddenly resented her for the freedom she enjoyed.

The next morning, Father was in the packed chapel at Whitehall. The palace was filled with all the nobility who had arrived for the queen's coronation, and everyone, it appeared, wanted to have it known they attended Mass, even though the queen was not present, due to her exertions of the previous day. When it was done, I returned with the women to the queen's quarters, and after we'd breakfasted, I set off to Father's rooms in a distant wing. There were more than a thousand rooms in the palace, a spreading maze of passages, but I eventually found my way there. His rooms were grander than mine, each with a fireplace, heavy furniture and colourful tapestries. His attendants, all known to me for years, greeted me with pleasure before he shooed them out so we could speak alone.

He told me he would be in London for only a few days, leaving before the queen's first Parliament met later in the week. "But tomorrow morning I've a private audience with her."

"You must tell her you want me to return home with you," I said assertively. "I can bear it here no longer!" To my utter amazement, I began to cry.

He observed me studiously, as if trying to determine whether my tears were genuine. Satisfied that they were, he poured me a cup of wine. He offered it to me, but when I shook my head he drank it himself and returned the empty cup to the table. He then brought me a linen napkin, with which I dried my eyes and blew my nose.

"Sit," he said, pulling a chair away from the table, into which I dropped. He remained standing before me, engulfed in the folds of a long, dark blue robe he'd changed into after Mass, the sleeves nearly covering his hands. "What is wrong?" he asked. "Yesterday I found you remarkably well adjusted to your new circumstances. This outburst surprises me."

"I detest it here!" I exclaimed. "The days are maddeningly boring and endless. Every day is the same, no matter where we are, here or at St James's Palace or Richmond Palace or the Tower! I rise early, dress in ridiculously monotonous clothing, join the silly gaggle of the queen's women — all of whom are so bland that they blend into one another — and go to Mass. Then we go to the rooms outside the queen's and are given something to eat, which must sustain us until noon. We sit and do nothing except watch the parade of visitors back and forth to the queen's room, usually the same old men. Then we go to dinner, eat so much we can barely move, and then go back to the queen's quarters and do nothing for the afternoon, until supper. And some days, we have to sit through Evensong, with music so mournful that it could be a dirge. That is what we do all day. For amusement, we can sew, play a few of the musical instruments scattered about, or play cards."

"You know how to play cards," Father said noncommittally. "And several instruments."

All the feelings I'd held back for the past two months had finally found an outlet, and I wasn't finished expressing them. "I have played so many times my fingers are raw! And I have to sit and smile politely while the geese-women tell me how good I am. Oh, it's so horrible! If I have to play one more instrument, I'll smash it, and if I sew one more lace handkerchief, I'll tear it to shreds!" My hands were clenched into fists, and I hit them together in frustration. "And the queen ignores us, except for Mrs Clarencius, the marchioness, and one or two other favourites, which I clearly am not. Oh, occasionally Mrs Clarencius will come out of the inner rooms and grandly select one of us to deliver a message." I scowled distastefully. "It's little better than being a servant. I have no one to talk to, except for the marchioness and my own gentlewoman attendant, Mrs Newton. Thank goodness for them — they alone save me from reduction to gibbering idiocy!"

Father was looking at me intently, but appeared unaffected by my complaints. "Has the queen met with you?" he asked. "Or spoken with you at any length?"

"Only once, the first night we arrived in the Tower of London. She called me to her after Mrs Clarencius told her I had learned the story of the two princes vanishing there. She was kind to me and apologised for not having paid me more attention. But since then there's been nothing more — an occasional gesture or acknowledgement on the way to Mass, or at dinner. Not a smile — she rarely smiles. It's as though she's telling me I'm just another of her gentlewomen, nothing special at all."

Father lifted one of his arms, tossing back the sleeve to hold up his hand, as if to say there was nothing to be done. Jewels flashed on his fingers; he wore at least three more rings than he usually did. He said calmly, "She has overwhelming duties to attend to. You haven't gone entirely unnoticed by her. Better not to be so prominent until matters have been better resolved, and she is more settled on her throne."

"I cannot endure it!" I nearly shouted, stamping my foot. "I want to go home to Skipton or Brougham! Or anywhere I'm not going to be treated as though it's my place to fade into the background. I should not be obscured the way I have been here, behind the Lady Elizabeth and Cousin Ned, both of whom are made much of. I am the granddaughter of a queen, and the great-granddaughter of a king! Was not my close cousin Jane just proclaimed a queen herself?"

"Lower your voice," Father said sharply. "You know better than to say such things. Or have you learned nothing here at court?"

His rebuke was correct; I did as he asked, but continued, "Was my mother regarded so in this very palace when her uncle King Henry reigned? I think not. And surely, she would not have her only daughter treated so now. Better for me to return to the north, where she went."

He turned away, went to the window, and stood looking out. Distantly, the sounds of voices in the courtyard below could be heard.

"I'm sorry for saying that," I said eventually. "And of course, I shouldn't have spoken so loudly or foolishly. The queen has been generous to me. But I want to go home."

He sighed and said wearily, "For me this place is replete with memories of your mother. The Great Hall where we were last night, the chapel we were in this morning, this entire wing holds them. Eleanor calls out to me from everywhere. It was the dazzling court of King Henry and Anne Boleyn then, full of wit, laughter and fashion. Eleanor made a great impression at it. She was never afraid in those years, always brave and bold and proud to be a Tudor. Do you know, she served as chief mourner when the deposed Queen Catherine died? None would come forward to do it out of fear of Anne Boleyn, none but her." He turned away from the window and back to me. "The queen remembers that. She remembers everyone who was kind to or honoured her mother during her troubles. She will favour you for it."

I went and stood beside him. "She fears me," I whispered. "I can feel it. She wants to be kind and generous, but somewhere within her she sees me as a threat. Better for me to be away from her, where she can't see me. I want to go home."

"Eleanor was never afraid here," he said distantly. "That came later, in the north."

I grasped his arms. "I'm not afraid, and I won't be, either here or at home. Father, I've done as you wished and stayed here for two months. We've demonstrated our loyalty to the queen. Surely she won't object if you request that I leave when you do."

The look on his face became urgent, pulling him back from his memories of my mother. "Do you think it was easy for me to leave you at Framlingham?" he asked, his voice controlled but harsh. "It felt as if I was leaving one of my limbs behind! I would like nothing better than to have your company again." He stopped and exhaled swiftly. "If I can, I will ascertain what the queen's mind is regarding this when I meet with her tomorrow. Possibly I will ask it of her. But I promise nothing. Unlike you, my daughter, I am afraid, although not for myself."

12

Late the next morning I was waiting for Father in his rooms when he returned from his audience with the queen. Although I hadn't seen him at dinner the day before — he'd dined at the home of the Earl of Shrewsbury — he'd been present for supper, after which we'd spoken, and he'd reiterated that, if possible, he would ask the queen if I could leave court. To me, it was as good as accomplished, and I'd gone so far as to speak to Mrs Newton about accompanying me home. But as soon as the door opened and I saw the preoccupied look on his face, I knew I was about to be bitterly disappointed.

Seeing me sitting there waiting for him, his lips compressed grimly. He said nothing as an attendant helped him out of his coat and took his feathered hat. "Go," he then told the man, who hurried out. He pulled out another chair and sat facing me. "You're to stay at court," he said.

It felt as if a door had just swung shut. The mere thought of remaining was almost unbearable. "The queen refused?" I managed to ask.

"No. I didn't ask her. After hearing certain things, I've decided this will be the safest place for you over the next few months."

Before I could protest, he stopped me with a swift wave of his hand. "Do not argue with me, Margaret! There is going to be trouble again, trouble that may possibly tear this country apart! The queen spoke to me of what will happen at this Parliament, which is about to open. First, a bill will be passed stating that the marriage of King Henry and the queen's mother Catherine was good and valid, so she will be legitimate again. The Reformers will detest this improvement in her status. Since it will leave Elizabeth illegitimate, it will appear to be a step toward excluding her sister from the succession. But even worse for them, all of the religious laws passed under King Edward are to be undone. The Mass will be restored everywhere, and the Book of Common Prayer is to be suppressed." He scowled, as though envisioning the chaos that would follow. "Her Majesty even wants to begin returning property to the monasteries that was taken in the time of her father. She says she is advised against it for now, but if she decides to proceed, it will bring turmoil. Her changes will not be accomplished easily, for she underestimates the depth of the Reformers' religious conviction. On her coronation day, the doors to the cells of Archbishop Cranmer and the others who were held in the Tower for defying the order to stop preaching, were deliberately left unlocked and unguarded, in the hope that they would escape and leave England. They chose not to do so. They will stay and struggle, and the queen will struggle against them."

Finally, I found my voice. "None of this has anything to do with me," I protested. "I've conformed to the old religion. I have avoided any discussions about faith."

Father's eyes widened. With anger, he said, "Child, do you forget the entanglement we have narrowly escaped from? There were those who sought to manipulate your royal position, your claim to the throne! And you were foolish enough to fall prey to the dazzling lure that was set before you!"

"My lord Father," I said angrily, rising, "you as well as I —"

"Sit down, Margaret," he commanded me, his tone so stern that I immediately complied. "The trouble we have escaped was brought on us by you. If you remember, I proposed a way of avoiding involvement with Sir Andrew Dudley, of shaking him off after his visit. You were the one who chose otherwise. If I am to be reproached for anything, it is that I did not struggle harder to dissuade you from agreeing to that marriage. You were foolish. It is why I have placed you here at court, not only so it will be harder for others to try to manipulate you under the watchful eyes of the queen and those who are devoted to her, but so that you can learn something of how to conduct yourself in this world where you will always be in danger. I have sheltered you away from the world for too long, as a comfort to me in my grief and disappointment. But I will not repeat that error, just as you must not repeat yours."

His words were as sharp as daggers, and I felt diminished by the onslaught. Never had he spoken so to me before.

He took another breath, and I braced myself for a fresh barrage of expressions of my failings. But when he spoke, he was calmer. "My concerns have almost caused me to forget to tell you this, and it is of the gravest importance. The queen confided that it is most unlikely she will marry the Earl of Devon — Cousin Ned. Not only does she find him unsuitable as a consort, despite his heritage, but she is considering marriage to another: her cousin Philip, the son of the emperor of Spain." He leaned forward and grasped both my hands. "Such a course would cause a great disturbance in this land. Both the Reformers and many of the old religion will be against it for fear of foreign powers. There will be plots, and some will try to take the throne from the queen, rather than see her so married. My daughter, you must guard against being drawn into such intrigues, and do nothing to rouse the queen's suspicions. She would not look with favour on your being taken from her care at this time."

His words had the ring of truth. That his overriding concerns were for my wellbeing and safety was unquestionable. But having my wishes denied was unfamiliar to me, and I tried one more approach.

"The queen has more cause to be suspicious of my Aunt Frances and her husband, and my cousins Catherine and Mary. Yet they are allowed to be at their homes." It was impossible to keep the resentment out of my voice.

"They are at Sheen, close to London. The dangers you represent as an heir to the throne would be from the north, which has always been more difficult to control. That was why my marriage to your mother was approved by King Henry, who well understood the benefit of a Tudor presence above York. Even so, the Pilgrimage of Grace was unavoidable." He paused, as though another thought had occurred to him. "I find it odd, Margaret, that you haven't asked if the queen mentioned the fate that will befall your cousin Jane? Is it of no concern to you?"

"Of course it concerns me!" I replied, offended.

"She will be tried in a few weeks and convicted. The queen will pardon and then release her, but not until she is herself married, and hopefully with child." Again, he hesitated before saying, "The remaining Dudley men will also eventually be pardoned, including Sir Andrew. But I assume I do not need to tell you to put him as far from your thoughts as possible?"

"I have." It was true; he seldom crossed my mind. But now, suddenly, I remembered the rich things he had sent in anticipation of our marriage. "What has happened to his property? All the riches he sent to Skipton?"

"I brought the jewels and some of the clothing with me and gave them to the queen. I await her instructions regarding the rest." His eyes fixed on my face for a long moment. "I find it curious also that you do not enquire as to how things are at home. You ask about property, but not about Mrs Brograve or your other women, who tended you for years. It is disappointing."

A variety of angry replies formed in my head, but all were countered by the overriding thought that he had merely pointed out the truth. However, I was in no mood to acknowledge this. With as much dignity as I could muster, I stood and silently left the room.

Somehow, I found my way back to the queen's quarters. In a passageway just within them, I encountered Mrs Newton. She took one look at my face and asked with alarm if I was all right. I told her I was fine and made my way into the anteroom, where the other women were scattered. I chose a chair near the centre, seated myself, smoothed down my russet dress, and folded my hands.

At first, I was adamant I would not bid Father farewell when he left, but Mrs Newton prevailed upon me to do so, and in the end, we even rode with him as far as Aldgate. But as we trotted along the London streets back to Whitehall, followed by the guards Mrs Clarencius had dispatched to accompany us on the queen's orders, Mrs Newton noticed the tears I had withheld until he was gone. "Change is the way of life, my lady," she said.

I remembered Father telling me months ago that the stars had foretold a time of change for me. "Do you think the stars control our destinies?" I asked.

"I believe God put them there as guides for people's lives, the same way sailors use them to find their way at sea. But you can choose which ones to follow."

I wished I had asked Father what guidance the stars were offering the queen, but it was a question that would have to wait until I saw him again. Although I would write to him, there were certain things it would be best not to commit to paper, especially if what he had predicted about upcoming discord and turbulence came to pass. One never knew who might be reading our letters, and that such a concern would even cross my mind surprised me. Perhaps I was becoming more aware of the dangers life held for me, as Father desired.

When we reached the palace, I asked Mrs Clarencius to please alert me when London merchants would next be displaying wares for the queen's household. "In particular, fine cloths and garments. I wish to have gifts sent to the women who cared for me at home."

I saw the first sign of the troubles Father had predicted a week later, after Parliament opened, when the marchioness barely spoke for an entire morning as we sat together outside the queen's room. At dinner, she sat beside the queen and chatted as usual, but her cheerfulness seemed forced, and several times I saw her stare ahead, as though her thoughts were elsewhere.

That afternoon, when Bishop Gardiner entered the anteroom on his way to the queen, she rushed across to him. He looked even more grim and dour than usual, frowning during their exchange, while the marchioness's hands fluttered with unusual agitation. Then the marchioness, twisting one of her rings distractedly, returned to my side, and the bishop, drawing his shoulders back, proceeded toward the closed doors of the queen's rooms. They opened and closed behind him as though he'd been swallowed. Despite her diminutive size, the queen was proving herself capable of dominating a court of powerful advisors. If she'd decided God wanted her to marry

Philip of Spain, she would have her way, regardless of the objections of the Bishop of Winchester, or the Marchioness of Exeter, or Parliament, or the people of her country.

The marchioness seized her needlework and seated herself. Then she said distractedly, "My son needs but time to overcome his failings."

Clearly, she'd spoken a thought aloud, and I knew no reply was expected. She then added in a bitter voice that I'd never heard from her before, "What else would one expect after ten years in the Tower?"

Her needlework hoop dropped to the floor, but when she made no move to retrieve it, I did.

"Thank you," she said as I placed it in her hands, which were trembling slightly. Without quite looking at me, she said distantly, in the same bitter tone, "The English will never accept a Spanish husband for the queen. Parliament needs to fight to prevent it." Determination crossed her face. Then, her attention shifted, and her weary blue eyes fell on me. She smiled politely, and in her usual perfectly smooth and measured tone, she said, "Parliament has just acknowledged the validity of the marriage of the queen's parents. It is a great victory for her. The hand of God is visible in it." Her eyes drifted away from me. "Or so she believes," she added, a hint of hardness creeping back into her voice.

She then began to apply herself to her needlework, until a disgruntled-looking Bishop Gardiner emerged from the queen's room. Once again, the marchioness conferred with him before he departed. Some time later, when other members of the Privy Council arrived in the anteroom, she swooped over to speak to them.

Cousin Ned's disappointment had been evident, although while his mother had sprung into action, he had at first retreated into sullen silence. For two weeks he was absent from court, until the queen pointedly told his mother that he was missed. That afternoon he appeared in the presence room, where the queen sat on her throne and formally received visitors to court or made official announcements. As he made his way down the long aisle after the usher announced him, the crowded courtiers on both sides scrutinised him mercilessly. But Cousin Ned didn't flinch beneath the unrelenting stares. Dressed in cloth of gold and his usual white velvet, a reminder of his descent from the House of York, he strode gracefully down the aisle, his handsome head perfectly positioned. Reaching the steps before the low dais on which the throne was set, he bowed with a flourish.

"Cousin, you have been missed," said the queen, her voice low-pitched but as loud as ever.

"Your Majesty flatters me with her notice," he said melodiously. "I have recently suffered a small melancholy."

"I am pleased to find you recovered," she answered. "My court was diminished by your absence."

He bowed again. Ahead of me, the marchioness started to applaud, and everyone else joined in, the nearby Bishop of Winchester and several other lords with great vigour. The sign of approval was not unnoticed by the queen. Her posture suddenly became rigid, and she glared toward the side of the room where the bishop and marchioness stood. I was glad I was farther back.

The presentation over, Cousin Ned retreated up the aisle and out of sight. Instead of watching him go, the queen beckoned one of the ushers and whispered to him. He dashed out, and a moment later the Spanish ambassador was announced. The ambassador began his walk down the aisle, greeted by cold stares and hostile expressions.

Cousin Ned stayed for supper, where he was seated in a place of honour beside his mother, who sat next to the queen. But afterward, he was seen for a long while in conversation with the Lady Elizabeth.

13

From that time, there was a distinct change in the mood of the court, a shift away from the buoyant feeling of victory and wellbeing that had surrounded the queen's arrival in London. Courtiers were not quite so jovial and spontaneous; everyone seemed to talk a little more quietly and was careful about what they said. Several nobles, either acknowledged Reformers or favourable toward them, were no longer content to remain respectfully silent, but left court, and there were rumours that some even planned to leave the country. Here and there I caught snatches of conversation and overheard remarks about the disapproval and bitter contention in Parliament over the queen's possible marriage to Philip of Spain. From Mrs Newton, I heard that there had been protests against the marriage among the citizens of London. One morning, we returned from Mass to find the ripped and shredded garments of a priest thrown about a corridor just inside the queen's apartments at Whitehall: a blatant statement of discontent, and a warning. But upon seeing them, the queen's face became even more set, and she only said, "May God forgive whoever has shown such disrespect to one of his chosen."

It was clear that the marchioness was continuing her campaign to influence members of the nobility and high-ranking officials to oppose the marriage. She had numerous whispered conversations, seemingly with anyone who would listen. Cousin Ned and the Lady Elizabeth continued to visit each other, often laughing and displaying a youthful gaiety, and both were seen in the company of the French ambassador.

The marchioness also was seen talking to the Lady Elizabeth. I remembered the distaste she had expressed not so long ago at having to carry her at her christening, and her constant references to 'the concubine' instead of Queen Anne Boleyn. Loyalties, it appeared, even very deeply seated ones, and ancient grudges, could easily be shifted and rearranged at court, especially when a throne or marriage to a queen was at stake. I marvelled at what seemed like an almost brazen disregard for the queen on the part of the Lady Elizabeth and Cousin Ned, but especially the marchioness, and wondered if they felt their positions were secure because of the widespread dislike of the queen's marriage intentions. But I also remembered how even infant children could be murdered if they stood in the way of a claim to the throne, and that being thwarted when success had stood so close might prompt one to recklessness.

Finally, the queen had had enough, and one morning the marchioness did not appear as usual. Mrs Clarencius told us she had been banished from court, her splendid suite of rooms taken from her. "The queen is disturbed by her lack of loyalty," she said, with an air of having been personally affronted as well. "The extent to which the marchioness has contrived to influence Parliament to reject her desired husband angers her." The women all exchanged looks of surprise. But no one said anything, and almost immediately all began to chatter about mundane matters. It was then that I understood my perception of them as a gaggle of silly geese was wrong: it was how they protected themselves from being drawn into intrigues.

Later in the day, Mrs Newton came to where I was in the queen's anteroom, sat beside me and offered a pair of gloves, as though to question me about them. "The Lady Elizabeth was visited this morning by two of the queen's councillors," she said surreptitiously. "It was some sort of warning not to be talking to the French ambassador."

I forced a smile. Pointing to one of the gloves as though I were speaking of it, I said softly, "You know the marchioness has been sent away from court?"

"Yes," she said. Smiling and letting out a little laugh as if I'd said something funny, she took the gloves and left.

An hour later, Mrs Clarencius came out to the anteroom and told me the queen wanted to see me. Silently I resolved to reward Mrs Newton handsomely for the timeliness of her warning about the Lady Elizabeth. With perfect poise I followed Mrs Clarencius into the queen's room, aware that all eyes were fixed on me as I went.

The room was dominated by a long centre table, at which the queen met with her council. No one was present but her, sitting at the far end, her head bent forward, her hands clasped together as though deep in thought, or prayer.

When I dropped to my knees beside her, she turned to face me. She looked tired and strained, with lines of tension around her blue eyes. Her usual French hood had been removed and was on the table before her, and her hair was pulled back.

"Lady Margaret. You are well, I trust?"

I replied that I was. She went on, "Mrs Clarencius tells me you have made quite a nice place for yourself among the women. You fit in very well. I am pleased to hear it." She pressed her lips together. "At least someone is content."

On the table beside her hood was a magnificent golden cross, covered with jewels, resting on a piece of blue silk. She picked it up and held it. "Could I trouble you to deliver this small gift to my si—" Before fully pronouncing 'sister', she stopped. "To Lady Elizabeth, with the simple message that it is a gift from me. Nothing more; she's had others very similar from me in the past. But it will have more meaning coming from one who is, like me, a Tudor."

She wrapped it in the silk and gave it to me. No other explanation was offered, no comment on what I already understood, thanks to Mrs Newtown: the gift was a sign that whatever explanations had been offered to her councillors, the queen had found acceptable. Less comprehensible to me was the reason for my selection to deliver the message. It could be a sign of solidarity with Lady Elizabeth, or a warning to her that others too had a claim to the throne. Or it could be a sort of test for me.

"I am pleased to be of help to Your Majesty," I said, and started to leave, walking backward as was required in her presence.

"You don't have to do that," she said, barely looking over at me. "Turn around and walk forward so you don't fall."

Just past the vacant rooms previously occupied by the marchioness were the Lady Elizabeth's rooms. She was writing at a table by a window in her bedroom when I was shown in by one of her women. Although most of the stoves and fireplaces in the palace were already in use, including the ones in the room I'd just passed through, hers were not. Neither did she wear a wrap around her shoulders, or a robe: she was seemingly oblivious to the coolness of the autumn air.

With a swift flourish, her hand swirled the quill over the paper, obviously signing her name. She then set it down, rose and came toward me, her longish oval face questioning, her slender hands clasped in front of her. Her long, red-gold hair was severely parted in the centre, and flowed down to rest upon the shoulders of her deep brown brocade gown. She wore no rings, and only one necklace, made of gold and diamonds.

She said nothing, so neither did I, merely extending the gift toward her. I felt unsure how to behave. We were cousins and had been in each other's company for several months, yet we had never exchanged more than a few polite words. Standing before her, faced with the perfection of her appearance, I felt awkward. My hair was never so sleekly arranged — stray strands always found their way out from beneath my hoods — and my black dress, although of the finest satin, looked dowdy compared to her stylish brown one.

She looked at what I was offering, her eyebrows lifting.

"A gift from the queen," I said.

She took it, unfolding the blue silk to reveal the jewelled cross. A half smile came to her face as she examined it. She then went to the window where there was more daylight, and inspected it again, dropping the silk on the table beside the quill and paper.

"A thing of beauty," I said, feeling some words were needed in the silence.

Ours eyes met, and I felt she was evaluating me. There was no hostility in her expression, only wariness and uncertainty. My face, I was sure, mirrored hers, and in that moment our mutual heritage seemed to surround us, allowing us to see in each other what we were unable to see in anyone else. I felt I should acknowledge this and say something of what I felt, but then I remembered that her woman had left the door ajar behind me after showing me in. Someone in the outer room could be listening. Earlier, I had wondered if I was being tested in some way; whatever I said might be reported back to the queen.

"A rich gift," I said. "The queen showed me before she wrapped it. When I first met her, she gave me a cross also. But it wasn't as large or as splendid as this one."

Lady Elizabeth's expression changed slightly, enough for me to see the barest trace of disdain in her widening smile. She then tossed the cross onto the table, on top of the blue silk wrapping. Our eyes met once more, hers still uncertain, reflecting my own feelings. Then she turned to the window behind her, indicating that the meeting was over.

On my way back, I encountered Mrs Clarencius emerging from the empty rooms of the marchioness. "She's gone," she said as she pulled the door closed behind her. "But who knows for how long? Queen Mary is so gentle and good, she forgives everyone." With a toss of her head, she indicated Lady Elizabeth's rooms. "She forgives everyone," she repeated, sourly. "Even that poor Lady Jane in the Tower, she's going to forgive. So the marchioness may be back here before long."

After little more than a week, the marchioness was received by the queen. Mrs Clarencius witnessed the reconciliation and told us, "She threw herself at the queen's feet and begged her forgiveness. I had to help the queen lift her back up. She's a lot heavier than she looks, and the queen is such a delicate little sparrow that she couldn't do it by herself."

The marchioness was reinstalled in her old rooms, which had been kept vacant. But she was no longer seated beside the queen at dinner and supper; instead, she sat with the other nobility. She also wasn't called in by the queen as frequently as in the past. Others also responded to her differently; the Lady Elizabeth barely acknowledged her, and Cousin Ned kept his distance during the infrequent times he appeared at court. As for myself, I tried to make sure others were close by when I sat with her.

Mrs Clarencius's words about the queen's forgiveness of the Lady Jane also proved prophetic. In the middle of November, she and her husband and two of his brothers were tried, convicted, and sentenced to death, as the duke had been. But all merely rejoined Sir Andrew in the Tower. The queen told her council that in time, she intended that they would be pardoned and released. It was, she said, the will of God for her to be merciful.

She also seemed firmly convinced that it was the will of God for her to marry Philip of Spain, something she made clear two days after the sentencing of Lady Jane, when Parliament formally petitioned her to marry only an Englishman. She received the deputation, led by Bishop Gardiner, in her presence room, before the entire court. Affronted, the queen flatly rejected it and told Parliament they had no right to interfere with her choice of husband. Bishop Gardiner went so far as to argue that as chancellor, it was his duty to present to her the extent of the dangers to England. "We may," he contended, "become a vassal state of Spain, like Naples and the Low Countries. We could also be drawn into Spain's wars with France!"

A murmur of approval ran through not only the members of the deputation, but the entire presence room. Visibly insulted and angry, the queen gripped the arms of her throne with her jewelled hands. It was no little sparrow but an eagle whose harsh voice told the bishop she would not marry someone simply because he was his friend. Immediately, Cousin Ned, his face frozen, detached himself from the crowd, stepped into the centre aisle, bowed, and backed out of the room. The bishop also bowed and did the same, followed by the deputation. All the while the queen sat rigidly on the throne, staring straight ahead, and remained so for several moments after the deputation was gone, while the court waited in utter silence. Across from me I saw the Lady Elizabeth standing as erect as a statue, her thoughts concealed behind a serene expression. Nearby stood the marchioness, her expression tragic, her eyes lowered to the floor.

Finally, the queen stood. "I wish to attend a Mass in my chapel," she said. She walked down the steps of the dais and up the aisle, everyone bowing as she passed. I hurried with the other women to follow her out.

Whatever lingering doubts the queen may have had regarding her choice of Prince Philip were then eradicated upon the arrival of his portrait from Spain. After viewing it alone for nearly an hour, the queen allowed her women in to see it.

There were gasps and exclamations of delighted approval as we entered. Full-sized and ornately framed, the magnificent portrait showed a handsomely fair young man, slim and elegant, with light brown hair and a beard, and gentle blue eyes set below a wide forehead. His posture was relaxed, yet sober and dignified. The queen stood before it, staring up as though enraptured. And I saw that from that moment, something more had been added to her decision to marry the young prince: the awakened hopes of an older woman who'd believed that life had passed her by.

I described the portrait to Mrs Newton, promising I'd do my best to let her see it before long.

"Is he much younger than her?" she asked.

"Eleven years. The same as Cousin … the Earl of Devon."

She started to say something but stopped. Even in the privacy of my rooms, we were both aware there were certain things that shouldn't be said. If we practised such caution when alone, we would be less likely to err in company.

"I had an aunt who was unhappily married for years," Mrs Newton confided. "Unlike the king, and the nobles, there's no divorce for people like us. You just have to stand it, even if the marriage was a big mistake. Or you can wait until the person dies — which is what my aunt did. But by then it was really too late for her. The only men she was interested in were much younger than she was, and she began to play herself for a fool. Finally, my mother told her in no uncertain terms that she was trying to recapture her lost youth, and it would never work. Once it's gone, it's gone, and you just have to accept that you're older." She gave me a meaningful look, her eyes wide. "I'm talking about my aunt."

"Yes, I understand," I said. A moment later, I added, "We'll see if I can get you in to see the portrait tomorrow."

Shortly after the arrival of the portrait, Lady Elizabeth left court. No one knew exactly why, since she only said she wished to spend time at her country estates. But there had been a change in her demeanour following the queen's rebuke several weeks earlier. Her attitude toward Cousin Ned, whose attention she had previously seemed to welcome, had altered completely following the change in the marchioness's status, and she avoided him. It was impossible to tell if she'd been disappointed by him or was fearful of showing how much she'd desired a match: such a marriage would strengthen both of their claims to the throne. Yet it was impossible to believe the queen would allow it until she had a child of her own to succeed her. Although Cousin Ned was staunchly of the old religion, Lady Elizabeth was but newly returned to it, and the queen couldn't yet be sure she would not go back to her Reformer views.

Lady Elizabeth, though, seemed much aware of the need to allay the queen's suspicions. Upon her departure, she requested the queen send her the necessary items for the saying of Mass in her home: as the chapel of a Reformer, it would have been devoid of ornamentation. Meanwhile, as a parting gift, the queen gave her a hood of sable, and a necklace of pearls.

I resented her departure, and as we assembled to wish her and her ladies farewell, I wished it was me who was leaving, returning to the north. Christmas was approaching, and I had always enjoyed the festivities at Brougham, when even my mother could be tempted from her rooms to participate in the cheer. The thought of my being absent from them was enough to bring me to tears, but I knew that petitioning Father would be useless. In many ways the Lady Elizabeth was in an enviable position; without a father or husband, she only had to answer to the queen. If I never married, I would eventually have a similar freedom, inheriting my mother's fortune and that of my father. I would be the sixteenth Lady Clifford, the twelfth Baroness Westmorland, and the third Baroness Vesci, one of the richest women in England.

But my most valued possession was my royal lineage, and I was determined to pass it on. To be married, and suitably so, was of the utmost importance.

14

A dark cloud hovered over the Christmas celebrations, the banquets and entertainments full of forced merriment. Even the New Year's Day exchange of gifts with the queen seemed stale. Using the overly generous allowance Father provided, I had purchased an elaborately jewelled gold cup for her. In exchange, I received cash, which I in turn gave to Mrs Newton. It was she who told me I'd received the largest amount the queen had given to any of her women, a sign of favour.

Right after the new year, the Spanish commissioners arrived to arrange the marriage treaty. As they represented the prince's father, the Holy Roman Emperor Charles, it was fitting that they be received by equally appropriate persons. The queen chose Cousin Ned, a clear attempt to mollify his wounded pride, and one court noblewoman: me. It was the first time I had been singled out for such a significant role, and I wondered if it was another sign of favour, or recognition of my relation to the royal family, or simply because I rode better than any of the other noblewomen at court. The London winter had been full of snow, the streets were treacherous, and it wouldn't do for there to be a mishap. The Spanish court was renowned for its sophistication, and it was important for the visitors to feel their prince was coming to a land befitting the son of an emperor.

The day of the arrival was gloomily overcast. We dismounted and assembled at the Tower river steps, where the commissioners would disembark. As we waited, I clutched my fur cloak tightly, since the breeze off the Thames was cold and damp. But Cousin Ned didn't bow his head against it, or pull up his hood, as some of the others did. He showed no impatience, but after some moments, he looked bored. He glanced about, as though seeking relief from it, and his large blue eyes came to rest upon me. He approached, and I expected him to express some polite remark about the weather. Instead, he gestured toward the Tower behind us and said, "The Lady Jane is now allowed to walk in the gardens."

Others were close enough to be listening. I replied evasively, "The queen is merciful."

"It is only a matter of time until the queen releases her, even if she does not disavow her Reformer beliefs — which I have heard she has not. I am told she spends her days reading Reformist works." He spoke with strange formality and remoteness, and unexpected pauses, all of which was likely the result of so many years in isolation in the Tower.

"Time must pass slowly in such circumstances," I said.

"The Duke of Northumberland converted back to the old religion."

He was moving toward subjects I wanted to avoid. "He did," I agreed.

"The other Dudley men will have done the same."

"Perhaps," I said, with as disinterested a tone as I could manage.

Suddenly he laughed, as though thoroughly amused. "Perhaps," he repeated. "Oh, yes. Perhaps." He then said something in a language I didn't understand.

I asked if it was Greek. "I remember you and my father conversed in Greek at the queen's coronation. But I'm afraid I don't understand it."

He looked genuinely shocked. "Really? I thought everyone knew Greek. Please accept my profound apologies. My comment was about the unexpected vicissitudes of life."

"Yes, life is full of surprises." There was another awkward pause. To fill it, I added, "I do read and speak Latin. But I doubt I do so as well as you."

"I studied the ancients while I was there." One of his gloved hands flicked toward the Tower behind us. "Unlike the Lady Jane, I had no interest in the works of the Reformers."

"I haven't read them. But during the reign of King Edward, we conformed to the changes, of course."

"You were betrothed to one of the Dudley men?"

It was the first time anyone had asked me about it since my arrival at court. Delicately, I answered, "Not formally betrothed. It all happened so quickly. The king wanted me to marry him."

"There was no contract?"

"No," I said emphatically. I now understood how wise Father had been to avoid such a commitment. If there had been one, it would have allowed for legal challenges to any later marriage that came to pass.

Other similar questions were prevented by the appearance of the Spanish commissioners. As we went through the formal welcome we'd rehearsed, I wondered why Cousin Ned had brought up my former betrothal. I hadn't expected him to know about it. He'd probably learned of it from his mother, and it would not have surprised me if they'd thought of me as a possible bride for him after he'd been rejected by the queen and Lady Elizabeth. They were, though, foolish in the extreme if they even considered such a matter without the consent of the queen, something I doubted would be forthcoming for a long while.

The passage through the London streets to Durham House where the commissioners would stay was unpleasant. The crowds that gathered as we passed were disapprovingly silent, except for angry mutters and occasional jeers. It was with relief that we rode through the Strand gatehouse to Durham House. The crowds' reaction had probably displeased the commissioners, but hopefully their accommodation would make a more favourable impression. Durham House was palatial and beautifully appointed. The Great Hall, where the Spanish ambassador greeted his newly arrived countrymen, was cathedral-like, with marble pillars and colourful tapestries.

The ambassador, clearly concerned, drew Cousin Ned aside and whispered to him. He in turn spoke to two attendants, who hurried away. To me, he said, "The chapel isn't appropriately furnished. This house was once owned by Northumberland."

It was then that I remembered Durham House had been where Lady Jane's and the other weddings had taken place less than a year ago. I thought of the young brides and grooms, full of hopes for a future so different from the one they had met.

Cousin Ned remarked that I had suddenly become pensive. "The Lady Jane was married here," I told him. "And the others. The two Catherines — her sister, and the duke's daughter."

"Northumberland married his daughter to Lord Hastings' son, did he not? Another scion of the house of York." He sniffed. "Not of kingly descent, though, merely from the Duke of Clarence. Royal, but not kingly, like us, being descended from King Edward IV. I've made a study of this. It's important for those like us to understand our background, to know exactly where we fit in." He smiled in a way that made me uncomfortable.

Seeking a change of subject, I said, "Only recently did I learn of the disappearance of the two young princes in the Tower, the sons of Kind Edward IV. I hear it's a mystery, what happened to them."

"They were killed," Cousin Ned said flatly. "They were in the way." With no emotion whatsoever, he added, "They were too young to fight back."

We were interrupted by the Spanish commissioners, who wished to present us with gifts. "In recognition of your close relation to the queen, and in acknowledgement of the graciousness of your hospitality today," one said in heavily accented English.

My gift was a small brooch of gold, with several star-like diamonds. Cousin Ned was given a golden ring, also set with diamonds. Both of us replied in the few Spanish words of gratitude we'd been taught for the occasion, as a sign of respect.

When it was time to leave, the captain of the guards who'd accompanied us explained it would be preferable to return to Whitehall Palace by the river, to avoid any hostile crowds that may have lingered on the streets. Barges for the short trip were already waiting at Durham House's river entrance.

On the barge, Cousin Ned sat across from me. Gradually a look of discontent came over his face, which then sharpened into a sneer. He removed his glove, slid the ring given to him by the commissioners from his finger, and surreptitiously dropped it into the river.

The following week, Bishop Gardiner announced to the court that the marriage treaty had been concluded. He presented the main terms, emphasising that although Philip would be called king, he would have no direct power, nor right of inheritance should the queen die without children. Philip, whose father would grant him the kingdoms of Naples and Jerusalem to give him the status of king to equal the queen's, was to arrive in a matter of weeks, and the wedding would take place before Lent.

Everyone in the presence room applauded, and the queen sat on her throne with a look of great contentment. But when she left, accompanied by the bishop, a wave of agitated whispering rippled through the crowded room, and the smiles were replaced by looks of concern. The unrest on the streets of London had been noticed by all. The treaty's intent of quelling suspicion and fear of England's absorption into the Spanish empire hadn't succeeded at court, and no doubt would fail also with the people. The speed and apparent urgency of the wedding preparations also caused comment: clearly, the queen and Philip wished to be married before their union could be prevented.

The subsequent departure of the Spanish commissioners did little to ease the tension that had taken hold of the court. The queen alone appeared pleased with the course that had been set by the treaty. The anticipation of her marriage had worked a change even upon her physical appearance, and she appeared younger, quicker and easier in her movements. The portrait of the prince seemed to enthral her, and for long stretches of time she would stand staring up at it. The women who attended her most closely spoke of how she had taken to visiting it first thing in the morning and last thing at night. She had even been overheard whispering to it.

The remaining weeks of January were cold and full of snow, preventing any excursions even into the palace gardens. The court felt quieter than it had during the autumn, in the absence of the Lady Elizabeth and Cousin Ned, who had stopped coming after the marriage treaty had been agreed. The marchioness had taken to sitting silently in a corner with her needlework, instead of scurrying to speak with the queen's visitors as she had previously. I was pleasant to her but remained at a distance: her subdued demeanour suggested she was frightened. Of what, I could only imagine, but my thoughts would sometimes return to Cousin Ned's sneer as he'd thrown the ring from the Spanish commissioners into the Thames. His absence from the court, apparently unnoticed by the queen, seemed ominous to me.

My days were spent with the other women, mostly sitting uselessly just outside the closed doors of the queen's rooms, while Bishop Gardiner and the other councillors entered and left. My observation skills sharpened, and the hopes and ambitions, and successes and failures of those who came and went soon became easily readable. It was therefore immediately obvious to me that near the end of January a crisis had begun. I knew even before Mrs Newton whispered to me that there was talk of an uprising, and before Mrs Clarencius drew all the women together to announce it, and before the queen called me to her room to privately tell me our relatives were once again involved.

She barely looked up from the papers on the table before her when I entered. "The Duke of Suffolk has joined the traitor Sir Thomas Wyatt," she said in a flat, controlled tone, "on the condition that Jane once again be proclaimed queen."

I could not stop a gasp from escaping my lips. Noticing, the queen lifted her head, fixing her gaze on me. But then she looked back at her letter, apparently satisfied that I knew nothing of it.

"The Earl of Devon is also involved," she said. "And possibly the Lady Elizabeth. There are some, it would appear, who would prefer her as queen, to the Lady Jane. Others prefer the earl. And others, I am told, would prefer the Lady Elizabeth and the Earl of Devon together, as a married couple.

They wish to reign as king and queen. But they will not. I will remain as queen, and Prince Philip will be king." Abruptly, she pushed the papers away from her and raised both hands to her forehead, as though exhausted. "I pray to God to give me the strength to carry my burdens," she said hoarsely. "But at times I wish I'd been born a lowly creature on some farm in the wilderness. Am I to have no happiness in my life?" Her voice was full of despair.

I said nothing; any comfort I could have offered would have been inadequate. I doubted she'd intended to confide in me.

With a heavy sigh, she pushed her chair back and stood up, then slowly walked over to stand before the portrait of Prince Philip. "But one must trust in the plans of God," she murmured. She looked at the portrait silently, as was her custom. When she turned back to me, it was with a renewed vigour and determination. "Be careful, Lady Margaret," she said in a gentle yet dignified tone. "And trust in the ways of God. He will reward us for our faith."

As I left the room, I could only think of how wise my father had been in insisting I remain at court. Had I been removed from it, there was no telling who might have tried to draw me into the current conspiracy, or with what suspicion I would be viewed. With a creeping sense of dread, I wondered what the outcome of the crisis would be not only for the queen, but for her sister, Cousin Ned and Lady Jane.

In the following days the queen showed great courage and resolve as Sir Thomas Wyatt triumphed over the queen's forces on his approach to London; at Rochester, five hundred men defected to him. Although her councillors begged her to escape, the queen refused to leave the city. Instead, she appeared at the Guildhall and gave a rousing speech, defending her choice of husband, and promising it would never interfere with the independence of her subjects. The people in the hall cheered her, as did others in the streets, but Sir Thomas's march toward London continued.

One by one, the courtiers began to vanish. Any messenger was surrounded by the queen's women and fearfully questioned before being allowed to pass through to the queen. They said that despite the queen's heroic speech at the Guildhall, terrified Londoners were barricading their doors, dismantling their shops, and fleeing the city. Each report frightened the women even more, and Mrs Clarencius did her best to calm them. But by the time the rebels had entered the city and managed to fight their way toward the palace, the women were clinging to each other, crying, and wringing their hands. When arrows hit some of the windows, chaos erupted, with the few remaining courtiers and numerous servants running through the palace in panic, seeking an escape.

But right then, the door to the queen's room flew open and she emerged. "We must keep our faith in God!" she announced. She then boldly strode to a nearby balcony overlooking a central courtyard and stepped out onto it. Cheers went up from the citizens below, who had crowded into the palace grounds for protection.

Mrs Clarencius hurried right outside after the queen, but all of the other women cowered away from the open door to the balcony. Courage and pride seized me as I watched the queen, who had pulled a cloak over her nightdress and wore no bonnet. Still she stood boldly before her people, demonstrating her bravery and fitness to wear the crown. Telling Mrs Newton to stay back, I went as far as the doorway, although I lingered safely just inside it. The queen's voice sounded almost supernaturally resonant as she addressed the frightened crowd, calming their fears and assuring them the rebels would soon be defeated by her superior forces.

Returning inside, she saw me at the door. I was proud to have followed her, but when another shower of arrows pelted against the shuttered windows, the extent of the danger I'd been in was impressed upon me. My legs suddenly felt weak, and I might have fainted had not Mrs Newton swooped forward and led me away to my room, where I collapsed on my bed.

It was morning when I opened my eyes. "It's over," Mrs Newton told me at once. "The queen has won. The Londoners who Sir Thomas had thought would support him remained hidden behind closed doors, and before dawn he surrendered. He's in the Tower already, with some of the other ringleaders."

I was still dressed in yesterday's black velvet livery. Sitting up, I threw off the blankets Mrs Newton had covered me with. "What news of Lady Jane's father, in the Midlands?"

"He was found hiding in a hollow tree on one of his estates. He's already on his way to the Tower."

"He's doomed. How can the queen possibly forgive him twice? At least Jane wasn't involved in it. There can't be any worse consequences for her."

But, as it turned out, there were terrible consequences, which I learned of the night Mrs Clarencius came into my room, shortly after the court had retired. Her visit at such a late hour was unusual, and felt even more ominous when she asked Mrs Newton to leave. Once alone, she told me the death sentences passed on Jane and her husband last November were to be carried out the following morning.

She stood rigidly as she spoke, her hands folded in front of her. But the fixed look on her usually expressive face, and the wavering of her voice, betrayed how unsettled she was. "The queen understands this will cause as much grief to you as it will to herself," she said. "She wanted you to learn of it privately."

Somehow, I stayed calm in the face of the imminent monstrosity I was being told of. The queen's unwillingness to tell me herself was almost as horrifying: it spoke of unacknowledged awareness that it was wrong.

"The Spanish ambassador has insisted that all possible dangers to Prince Philip be removed before he arrives in England," Mrs Clarencius went on. "Jane and her husband would always be a threat. They must be permanently removed, by execution, or the marriage will not take place."

She paused, as though waiting for a reply. Futilely, I cast about for one. Certainly, it couldn't be the truth: I couldn't say that the queen was covering an infatuation with the younger prince by explaining it as God's will; that she was trying to reclaim her lost youth; and that she was seeking to avenge her wronged mother by creating the future that the long-dead Spanish queen had hoped for. It would be of no use for me to say this to Mrs Clarencius, or even to the queen herself, if I dared, for the portrait of Prince Philip had so enthralled her that it was not possible for her to make any other choice. Jane and her husband would die, as would Jane's father, and likely the Lady Elizabeth and Cousin Ned as well.

"God has twice now given the queen victory over her enemies," Mrs Clarencius said defensively, as though I'd argued. "She is good and merciful. Even now, at this late hour, she offered Lady Jane the chance of a pardon, if she would convert back to the old religion." Her eyes narrowed angrily. "She refused."

Of course Jane had refused; she was as convinced of the rightness of her beliefs as the queen was of hers.

Mrs Clarencius was still talking, although I no longer listened. I turned and looked at the window, seeing nothing but the cold winter night pressed against the glass.

Eventually, Mrs Clarencius fell silent and placed a hand on my shoulder. "Courage," she said, before leaving.

Mrs Newton returned, and I told her the news. Seeing her shocked expression, I said, "Most horrible is that the queen is a good woman." She started to reply, but I stopped her with a gesture. There were many things too dangerous to speak of, even to each other, and one of them was how terrible the consequences could be when those in power deluded themselves through religion.

My resignation kept me calm, a state of mind I managed to maintain throughout the executions. Other bleak news followed: Cousin Ned had been committed to the Tower, returned to the very rooms where he had spent so much of his life, and the Lady Elizabeth, already in custody, would likely soon follow him. The marchioness was banished from court, and this time her vacated rooms were reassigned immediately.

Jane's father was found guilty of treason only days after Jane died, and sentenced to death. On the day of the execution, I was in my usual place in the anteroom to the queen's council room, where a number of courtiers had gathered. The room became crowded, causing a little group of gentlemen to come close to where I was sitting. I was therefore able to listen in on their conversation.

I heard one say he had just come from the execution on Tower Hill. He started describing how the duke had died. "The fellow made a good end of it," he said. "Very dignified and courageous, and he spoke the way you'd expect from a duke. The beheading was smooth — he knelt easily in place, and it was done. Not at all like that poor daughter of his."

"Oh?" asked another. "What happened to Jane?"

"After the handkerchief was tied over her eyes, she couldn't find her way to the block. She stumbled about, asking where it was, until someone in the crowd stepped up to the scaffold and helped her. It was a heartbreaking scene, and brought everyone to tears."

Abruptly, I stood up, causing them to look at me. One whispered something to the others, and I heard the words "her cousin". They parted to create a path for me to leave, all bowing as I swept past them.

Back in my room, my calm and resignation finally deserted me, and I wept bitterly. The image of a blindfolded Jane struggling awkwardly toward her death was too much for me; I remembered only her perfect poise and precision, her delicately controlled gestures.

Her father's death caused me grief also, although I'd barely known the duke. Unlike Father, he'd been unable to shield his daughter from the dangers of her royal lineage, and it had destroyed them both. Possibly the pressures had been greater, the ambition and self-delusion more intense. Or maybe it had been twists of fortune that had preserved my father and me from sharing their fate.

Over the days that followed, I began to feel that more than fortune, it had been Father's wisdom that had kept us from harm, a wisdom that had prevailed despite my recklessness. The decision to place me in the care of the queen at court now seemed a brilliant calculation on his part. I resolved to let go of any lingering resentment I felt and make the best of it, even though the court was now even more unpleasant than I had found it upon my arrival. The marchioness, who had befriended me, was gone, and the executions cast a shadow over everything. The approach of the queen's wedding did little to dispel it. Mrs Newton even went so far as to comment to me, "No one builds happiness on the misfortunes of others."

Then I received a letter from Father:

Dear Margaret,

It was with great fear and concern that I heard the news of Wyatt's rebellion, which the Duke of Suffolk was foolish enough to join. And it was with equal relief that I heard of your safety, and that of the queen. It is also with sadness that I learned of the execution of the Lady Jane, who has fallen victim to her father's foolishness. His understanding of what he brought to pass must have been unbearable, and I believe he must have found death a welcome release. I can only hope that the Lady Jane's religion brought her some comfort.

I have had reports from various members of the queen's council that you conducted yourself admirably during the troubles, and I have received this news with pride and satisfaction.

Margaret, it is time I informed you of my intention to marry again. The queen suggested it during our meeting at Framlingham, stating it was my responsibility to produce a direct heir for the Cumberland earldom, which you know must be a male. As by now I am sure you understand, royal suggestions have the weight of commands, but I must admit I am not averse to it, as I previously would have been. A match has been proposed with Anne, the daughter of Lord Dacre, whose wife is sister to the Earl of Shrewsbury. The earl and I spoke of it at the queen's coronation, and I have considered it favourably during the months since then. Soon, I will visit Lord Dacre, and if Lady Anne and I like each other sufficiently, I am prepared to move forward.

Rest assured there will be no diminishment of the honour and love I have for you, and your mother, whose memory I hold sacred. But I now see how close to disaster we both came due to my clinging to you as a remembrance of her, keeping you from finding your place in the world. But

as you have moved on, it is time for me to set aside my mourning and
participate again in life.

I will write you more, as plans progress, if indeed they do. But I did not
want you to hear of this news from any other than myself.

Your loving father,
Henry Cumberland

I stared down at the letter in my hands, scarcely able to believe what I had just read. Any male child born to him would displace me from inheriting the titles and accompanying lands I had for years been expecting. All I'd have left would be my inheritance from my mother. But the feeling of loss now overwhelming me was larger than concerns of property, for it felt as if my past was about to be torn away from me.

Most revealing was the remark that the queen wanted him to marry. For her, my inherited titles combined with my royal lineage made me too much of a threat. So reduced, I would be less of a prize for another ambitious husband, like Sir Andrew Dudley.

My confidence in Father's wisdom vanished, replaced by the old feeling of betrayal. After the second revolt, the queen undoubtably felt more insecure on her throne, which she believed God wanted her to have. Almost immediately after Jane's father's execution, there had been talk that the queen believed his treason extended to his family, and she had permanently disqualified his wife and remaining daughters from the succession. The Lady Elizabeth's claim was already troubled by her illegitimacy, and even if she avoided execution or condemnation for treason for her involvement with Wyatt, it was doubtful she would be successful. That left only me with a clear claim to the throne, according to the succession acts of two kings, Henry and Edward.

The queen clearly was not going to allow me to marry. An appalling vision of endless days spent on the sidelines of court now appeared before me. I would grow old, fade away and die, forgotten by all, the threat of my claim to the throne vanished like dust in the wind. Meanwhile, life would go on at Brougham and Skipton, with new children taking the place of myself and my deceased mother and brothers. It would be as if I had never been born.

Deep within me, something revolted at the very thought of it. Defeat was not something any Tudor accepted easily, and it wouldn't do for me to surrender so meekly to such a fate. Both my life and my mother's would be rendered meaningless if I did so. Though my heritage and position had been reduced, I still had my wits. They were sharper now than they had been in the north, my time at court having been a useful school.

I would use them now to increase the queen's trust in me. It was questionable whether a woman of her age could successfully bear a child, but it would be the easiest way to secure my release from the shadow of her fears. And so I began to hope for the accomplishment of the queen's marriage, but for reasons of my own.

15

Near the end of May, the Lady Elizabeth and Cousin Ned were released from the Tower into the custody of gentlemen who would maintain them far from court, under watchful supervision. Cousin Ned had confessed minor involvement, but despite valiant efforts on the parts of numerous councillors, it had been impossible to prove Elizabeth's complicity in the rebellion. But it was clear the queen no longer trusted either of them, especially her sister. Privately, she began denying their relationship and took to referring to the Lady Elizabeth as 'Smeaton's daughter'.

"He was a musician who was one of her mother's many lovers," Mrs Clarencius smugly explained. "The concubine was executed for adultery."

The queen's remarks overlooked the physical resemblance between the sisters, which despite their difference in height and stature were striking, especially their red hair. Older courtiers also from time to time casually observed that of the two, the Lady Elizabeth resembled her father most closely. But the years of hatred the queen had suppressed for the woman who had displaced her mother, which the joy of successfully claiming the throne had held in check for the first months of her reign, had now been unleashed by her bitterness over the last revolt. Queen Catherine had been left vulnerable to Anne Boleyn's ambition because of her failure to produce a son. It was clear that now more than ever, the queen felt her security and future happiness rested on having a child. She now showed a new determination when she spoke of Prince Philip to others. It was clear that she believed the will of God needed to be applied with force, and any obstacles removed.

The day after the departure of the Lady Elizabeth and Cousin Ned, the Earl and Countess of Lennox arrived in London. The timing of the visit seemed to have been carefully calculated to make a statement: the countess was a Tudor, with what some saw as a strong claim to the throne, despite having been barred from the succession by King Henry. She and her husband had ties to France, currently in the middle of one of their incessant wars with Spain, and she had an eight-year-old son.

"She was the daughter of my aunt Margaret Tudor, the Queen of Scotland, from her second marriage to a Scottish earl," I explained to Mrs Newton after we'd been told of her imminent arrival. "She was half-sister to King James, and so is aunt to Mary Queen of Scots. Her husband has lands both in the north of England — on the other side from my family's — and in Scotland, where he has his own claim to the Scottish throne. So, the little boy — they call him Lord Darnley — has claims to both the throne of Scotland and England. But they were barred from the English succession."

"Why?" Mrs Newton's face showed confusion. "If Queen Margaret was older than your grandmother, shouldn't her children come first?"

"The countess is of the old religion and argued with King Henry over his changes. She'd been in the succession, but he took her out, in favour of my family. But she is also seen as illegitimate. King Henry went to great lengths to have her declared so, after both of his daughters were. The little Queen of Scotland was barred because she's a foreigner. She's of the old religion also."

173

Mrs Newton was kindly disposed toward others, always willing to view their motives as good until she learned differently. But nothing ever interfered with her common sense, which at times cut directly to the core of a matter. Her eyebrows now rose with disapproval. "Some who think God uses them for His purposes are really using Him for their own," she said. "It's not that they're bad people. They get confused when it's something they really want."

Growing up, I'd had the best tutors and read many of the great ancient writers. There had been lessons about life in them, most of which I'd not fully understood until my arrival at court, when suddenly they'd felt useful. But at times it seemed my contact with all the attendants and servants at Brougham had taught me lessons of equal value, things that couldn't be learned from books. Some people who'd had no education saw the truth more easily than those who had. I said, "My dear Mrs Newton, you have wisdom beyond your years."

She smiled, flattered. "The countess has connections to France," she answered pointedly.

"France and Spain are ancient enemies. The Queen of Scots is in France, where when she is old enough, she will marry the Dauphin. Her mother the regent of Scotland is French. And the Earl of Lennox's own family has French relatives." I paused. "Many in England now fear the arrival of the Spanish."

"The enemy of my enemy," she said, "is my friend."

"The earl and countess hope to make the most of the fear of Spain. There may even be those who still hope the queen can be influenced to stop the marriage. Mrs Clarencius told us that years ago the countess was one of the queen's great friends. But she doesn't know yet the extent of the queen's desire to marry Prince Philip."

"And the other reason they're here," Mrs Newton said, "is to remind everyone they have a son."

I looked at her knowingly but said nothing. I'd already given that child much thought, remembering the horrible suspicions my father had of the King and Queen of Scotland's roles in the death of my mother and brothers, and of my grandfather's revenge on their sons. The countess, being King James's half-sister, could have been involved, or at least had knowledge of it. Whether she had or not, she now had an eight-year-old son with Tudor lineage who had escaped the possibly sinister fate that had claimed all his male cousins. It was an accomplishment that could be the result of shrewdness, luck, or the hand of God. No matter what one attributed it to, it would not be wise for me to speak to Mrs Newton or anyone else of Father's suspicions.

Those suspicions were on my mind the next day as I watched the earl, the countess and their son walk down the aisle of the presence room toward the queen. The earl was as handsome as the countess was beautiful, both with fair golden hair, blue eyes, well-balanced faces, and tall, imposing figures. The young Lord Darnley, walking between them with perfect grace, had inherited the same excellent features from both. All three were dressed in black silk, clearly expensive but with minimal ornamentation, almost Reformer-like. The only jewellery visible beyond the wedding rings of the parents were the gold crosses worn by all three, shining prominently against the black silk.

They reached the queen and bowed in perfect unison, which was clearly practised. The queen rose from her throne and went to them, her arms outstretched, saying, "Welcome! Welcome, dear cousins!" Her voice sounded even deeper than usual. From behind, I saw Lord Darnley's head jerk upward, startled by it. Both of his hands rose, as though he were about to cover his mouth to control laughter. Instantly, one of the countess's hands landed firmly on his shoulder, and his posture stiffened as his arms dropped back down to his sides.

The queen embraced the countess first. From behind we saw her arms encircle her slightly above her waist, emphasising her shortness beside her statuesque cousin. They shifted positions, and the queen suffered even more by comparison, looking like a child not much older than Lord Darnley.

"Praise God Your Majesty has been preserved from the traitor Wyatt, and the treachery and ingratitude of those who conspired with him," said the countess.

Unlike the smooth beauty of her appearance, her voice was unpleasant, carefully controlled but with a shrill, aggressive tone. Her words sounded clipped and sharp.

"Yes," agreed the earl, and in the one word, I heard the same tone I'd heard from his wife, and knew the rest would be the same. The impression of seamless attractiveness had for me shifted into a duplicitous veneer. These people were wolves, as beautiful as the white ones of Europe I'd heard of, and as ferocious.

"Praise God," said Lord Darnley, bowing his head. In Latin, he murmured the first lines of a prayer; I could hear they had something to do with vanquishing traitors. Pleased, the queen complimented his scholarship and reached out and tousled his golden hair. Instinctively, he shuddered, as though her jewelled hand was a threatening claw, and his face showed disgust. But abruptly it shifted to an angelic expression. He smiled up at the queen and said, "I study my books to honour you, Your Majesty."

The court applauded, and the queen, pleased, patted his head. This time, his expression didn't alter. His voice had held traces of the same tone I'd heard in his parents' voices. Clearly, he was a cub that would grow into an equally dangerous wolf.

"Let me show you my future husband," the queen said as she started leading them away. "I mean, his portrait — he's not here yet." I wondered how much effort it would take for the three of them to refrain from pouncing upon the portrait and tearing it to shreds.

They were given the suite of rooms vacated by the marchioness, near to my own. It wasn't fair of me, I told myself, to have so negative a reaction to them; I would have to try not to be so influenced by what Father had told me, which hadn't even been about them. They were, after all, my cousins, and I had no proof that the countess and earl had ever acted dishonourably. But there was something unnerving about them. The charming veneer and polished manners seemed to conceal a wild ambition. I noticed too many moments of unusual alertness on their part, too many frozen smiles and unexpected questions.

They were often with the queen when she was not with her council or attending to state business. They sat beside her on the dais during dinner and supper, or ate alone with her in her rooms. When not with her, they were engaged in an endless stream of meetings, both in their rooms at Whitehall or elsewhere in the city. They made as blatant a statement as possible of their commitment to the old religion, attending Mass twice a day and seeking out the most religiously conservative members of the court. I noticed that they often managed to make sure the queen saw them in such company.

Shortly after their installation in the marchioness's old suite, we began to notice smells of cooking coming from their rooms. "The countess's women say they cook for the little boy in there," Mrs Newton told me. "The countess goes to the kitchens and selects food, or sometimes out of the palace to the market. The rest of them eat at the common table with everyone else, even the earl and countess. But they won't let the child eat there."

Over the next few days I watched and saw that Lord Darnley sat quietly at his father's side during dinner and supper, but never touched food or drink. Uncomfortable memories returned to me, of my mother doing the same at Brougham, as well as preparing food in her rooms. I'd been too young at the time to understand that she'd been afraid of being poisoned. But now, I little doubted this was the reason why Lord Darnley was being fed in such a protected manner. My suspicions that the countess had knowledge of prior murders soared. Why else would she feel her own child was vulnerable?

One morning several days later, I returned to my rooms after Mass. The queen was in formal conference with her Privy Council and the earl and countess regarding policy toward Scotland. There was little chance I'd be called on for anything for the rest of the morning, so I decided to go back to my rooms. Even so, I asked Mrs Newton to remain and fetch me if needed.

As soon as I entered my outer room, I heard the muffled sounds of arguing beyond the wall separating it from the earl and countess's suite. It grew louder, the childish voice of Lord Darnley distinct. I heard a distant door open and slam shut, followed by running footsteps. Then the door to my room flew open, and Lord Darnley entered. Quickly but quietly, he closed the door behind him and pressed his back against it.

"Don't say anything!" he whispered, pressing a finger to his lips. Then, from the corridor there were the sounds of adults, arguing and running past my door. Clearly, they were seeking him, and he'd found a haven in my room.

His face was wet with tears. Once the footsteps vanished, he relaxed and exhaled.

"I'll remember," he said unpleasantly.

"Remember what?"

He then seemed to see me for the first time. "I'm Lord Darnley," he said grandly. "The queen is my cousin."

"She's my cousin too. And that would make us cousins as well."

He stared at me suspiciously. "You're not," he said dismissively. "And we're not."

I couldn't help but laugh at his belligerence. "What reason would I have to tell you an untruth?"

"Don't you dare laugh at me," he said angrily. With his thumb, he gestured behind him to the corridor outside the closed door. "That's what they just did. They won't get away with it. I've already punished them by running away. My parents tell them never to leave me alone. They'll have them all whipped for letting me get away." He folded his arms and smiled with satisfaction.

"That won't be a very nice thing, will it, Lord Darnley? People in our position should always be respectful of those who attend us."

"What do you mean, *our* position? You think you're very important, don't you?" He peered at my face. "I know who you are. You're that Clifford woman, aren't you?"

"I'm Lady Margaret Clifford. Our grandmothers were sisters."

He snickered. "You're one of those Clifford dogs."

Shocked, I said, "That is a very rude thing to say!"

He laughed. "That's what my father calls the Cliffords. 'Dogs, all of them,' he says."

Never in my life had anyone spoken to me so. No attendant or servant would have dared. But here I was, being confronted by someone of equal status, who even at his young age should have known better. "It is you who should be whipped, not your servants. I will tell your mother."

"Go ahead. She won't do anything. She doesn't like you."

It was unsettling to hear it so expressed. The countess and I had been presented to each other on the day of her arrival by the queen herself. Both she and the earl had been gracious and pleasant, but I had immediately sensed a concealed hostility.

The child was now staring directly into my face, scrutinising it with the fearful look of a cornered animal. "She says you're dangerous," he said, his eyes narrowing. "She says all the Cliffords are dangerous. I'm to stay away from you. And I would have, except that I needed somewhere to hide."

Uncertainty was creeping over him, his bravado vanishing. Suddenly, despite being appalled by what I'd just heard from him, I felt an overwhelming sympathy for the child. He looked very small and frightened now, almost crouching back against the door.

"I'm not at all dangerous," I said gently. "I can assure you that you have nothing to fear from me. Not all dogs bite; some are very sweet and kind."

Some of the fear left his face. I had no experience with children, but I sensed he might find me less threatening if I sat down. Moving slowly, I sat in a chair by the window. There was now more space between us, and our eyes were on the same level. "Do you wish to sit down and wait for your attendants to return?" I asked.

He didn't move. "No," he said. "I don't want to go back in there yet. It's like a cage. I hate being at court."

"I hated it too when I first got here. I still don't like it, but it's not so bad now as it was then. You get used to it."

A dull look came into his eyes. "Our home at Temple Newsam is almost as big as this palace. I have rooms all to myself, and they're full of my things. We're not all stuck together the way we are here. It's not as bad, even though everyone is still watching me all the time. They're always telling me to stand up straight, or making me speak in French, or having me practise some screeching instrument. Mother and Father are always saying, 'a king does it this way,' or 'a king would never do that!' They think I'm going to be a king someday."

"And how do you know that?" I asked.

"It's in the stars."

"Your parents told you?"

He shook his head. "I heard them talking to an astrologer. They don't know I did, but you could guess it anyway, from the way they treat me."

"The stars only incline," I said. "They don't compel."

He ignored me. "It's why they want me to be perfect," he went on. "And I try, most of the time." He hesitated. "But there are some days when I just want to smash everything in the room I'm in." He lifted his hand, clenching it into a fist. "Smash, smash, smash!" he said, punching the air before him.

He then leaned away from the door and shook his shoulders and arms, recovering his poise. "I'm going to leave now," he said politely. "Thank you for your hospitality."

"Lie down and pretend you're asleep when they come back in," I offered. "And then say you were there all the time, and they just missed you. We won't need to tell anyone you came in here."

A look of contempt came over his handsome young face, his lips pursing. "I'm not afraid, Lady Margaret. Are you?"

He opened the door and left. I listened to the sound of his receding footsteps in the corridor.

I was still sitting in the same place when, a short while later, I heard more footsteps and voices in the corridor, and then the door to the earl and countess's suite open and close. I waited for the sounds of arguing, but there were none. With the tiniest sense of satisfaction, I understood that the child had likely done as I'd suggested and pretended to be asleep when the attendants returned.

Later, when Mrs Newton came in search of me to go down to dinner, I still hadn't moved. "I lost track of time," I said apologetically.

"What have you been doing?" she asked curiously.

I didn't reply. There were things too dangerous for us to speak about, even to each other.

16

Shortly before midsummer the Spanish ambassador spent several long hours with the queen. He entered the meeting looking very determined and angry, but left smiling contentedly. Afterward, the queen sat alone for a long while before the portrait of Prince Philip. She then called the countess and earl to her, from which meeting they emerged looking crestfallen. That evening, it was announced to the court that they would be returning to their home in the north. When they left the next morning, the only one who seemed happy to be going was Lord Darnley.

After their departure, preparations for the arrival of Prince Philip, who was expected in a month, immediately began to dominate the court. An entire household of more than two hundred attendants mirroring the queen's had already been chosen for him, and they were made ready to receive him at Southampton. The leading members were presented to the queen before departing. The queen's women all watched with interest as the gentlemen selected as his closest attendants passed through the anteroom on their way to her. All were fashionably dressed, handsome, and mostly young. "The queen ordered that special care be taken in choosing them," Mrs Clarencius told us, after they'd gone in. "They are the sons of the most important noblemen in the kingdom. Some of them were in attendance on King Edward and grew up with him. They know what is required for a king. Of course, they've returned to the old religion now."

The women all began to chatter excitedly, but I turned away and went back to my usual seat. The mention of King

Edward's gentlemen had reminded me of Sir Andrew Dudley, still in the Tower with his nephews. They had escaped execution, but their ultimate fate was still uncertain. I knew that before Sir Thomas Wyatt's rebellion the queen had intended to release all of them, with Jane and her husband, once her marriage had been successfully accomplished, but I'd heard nothing since. I certainly couldn't enquire about it without appearing to still have an interest in marrying Sir Andrew, which I did not. The man had sought to use me to realise his ambitions, which I now resented. But I also couldn't deny that I had been willing to use him to realise my own. It was a mistake I had escaped from, and it seemed right that Sir Andrew should escape also. But there was nothing I could do to help him.

It was at Winchester, in the bishop's palace, that the queen was to first lay eyes on the man whose portrait had so captivated her. King Philip — the Kingdom of Naples having been gifted to him by his father upon his setting foot in England — was to present himself to her late in the evening on the day he arrived from Southampton. Only a handful of courtiers would be present, since the queen wanted the first meeting to be quiet and private. She also wanted it to be at night, an excusable vanity which perhaps only her women understood, for by candlelight she appeared younger and softer than she did in the harsh light of day. To prevent her suffering by comparison, the few women selected to accompany her were older ones, with one exception — me.

I was honoured to be chosen, and said as much to Mrs Clarencius when she brought me the news. "She likes you," was her simple reply.

"You're her nearest relative at court now," Mrs Newton added when we were alone. "You should be included."

I doubted the stately, sombre rooms of the bishop's palace had ever seen such excitement as filled the place when the scheduled day arrived. A vast number of the queen's gowns had been brought from London, and the women fluttered around, offering opinions on the merits of each. The excitement increased with reports of the king's progress along the ten-mile trip to Winchester. He had left Southampton with an enormous retinue in the pouring rain, still impressively attired in white satin, a red cloak and many jewels. Just outside Winchester, he had stopped and changed into black and white velvet laced with gold thread. Entering the city, he'd gone directly to the cathedral, where he'd been welcomed by Bishop Gardiner and other notable bishops, who'd sang a Te Deum. Afterward, he'd gone to his nearby quarters to rest and dine, before meeting the queen.

The queen dispatched one of her new Spanish-speaking servants to try to discover what he would wear at their meeting. He returned, beaming with satisfaction at his success, and reported that it would be blue satin, chosen because he knew it was her favourite colour. Hearing this, tears of joy came to the queen's eyes, and she whispered, "Such kindness." She covered her face with her trembling hands.

For the next hour, the women argued over which gown would best compliment the king's blue satin. Finally, they decided on a high-necked gown of black velvet and silver. The high neck was important because, although no one said it, everyone saw that the queen's age showed most there, despite applications of beeswax and sesame oil. Numerous rings, bracelets and necklaces were then added. Two or three of the women, newer to the queen's service and unused to dressing her, suggested she wear none, but were ignored, because the others understood the queen's penchant for jewellery had much to do with seeing it as a replacement for the lost sparkle of youth. An English-style bonnet was then selected, a departure from the French ones she favoured. For at least the first several meetings, everything French was to be avoided, a gesture of respectful recognition of Spain's ancient enemy. The Countess of Lennox and her family, with their French connections, had been sent away for the same reason.

At the end, one final touch was added: Mrs Clarencius dipped a cloth in water coloured with red ochre and very lightly touched the queen's lips with it. All the women then voiced their approval, and the queen retired to the palace chapel to spend the remaining time before the meeting in prayer.

Shortly before the appointed time, we accompanied her to the long gallery. To my astonishment, her earlier girlish agitation was gone, and she stood waiting with statue-like calm and dignity. When footsteps were heard approaching in the corridor, she along with the rest of us looked toward the door, but turned away when it became clear it was only one pair of feet, and certainly not the king, who wouldn't be unaccompanied.

An unknown gentleman entered, dressed in Spanish-style clothing, and whispered to one of the new Spanish-speaking attendants, who then in English reported that the king was on his way, crossing the garden. The queen became utterly still. I felt a rush of sympathy for her; she had been plagued by loneliness her entire life, and now she was grasping at her last chance of happiness — something she'd sacrificed in her struggle to reach the throne.

We heard footsteps in the corridor again, this time with accompanying voices. Suddenly the tension proved too much for the queen, who lost her composure and nearly ran to the door. Just as she reached it, King Philip appeared in the doorway, the living image of what proved to have been a remarkably accurate portrait. His hair and beard were fairer than they'd been painted, closer to yellow than brown; otherwise, everything about his appearance was as expected.

Seeing the queen, he smiled without the slightest pause, stepped forward, and kissed her on her red-tinted lips. She tottered in surprise, but he took her by the hand, steadying her, and led her to where two thrones were waiting beneath a canopy of state. Everyone bowed or curtsied as they passed. I was close enough to see that his eyes, blue in the portrait, were closer to grey. His face was self-assured and determined, while the queen's expression was one of great happiness and slight disorientation. I doubted she'd even noticed that his clothing wasn't the expected blue satin, but white kid, with a coat embroidered with silver and gold.

We remained at a respectful distance as they sat on their thrones and talked. We knew they were speaking in Latin, the only language they shared, but we were too far away to hear their conversation. Beside the king's sophisticated and easy manners, the queen looked naïve and awkward, restraint showing in the rigidity of her posture. But as their conversation continued, she leaned toward him steadily. Several times, he responded to her remarks with a very refined, bemused smile, and her face showed satisfaction.

After a while, he took her hand again, and they stood up. He beckoned to one of his gentlemen, who approached and conferred with him. The gentleman then spoke to one of the interpreters, who came and told us the king wished to take the queen back to the garden he'd just passed through. Servants carrying torches appeared and led the way, followed by the king and queen, and then the rest of us.

Outside the garden was fragrant, with trees rustling and the torches flickering in the light breeze. The king and queen spoke together quietly, and I was close enough to catch occasional Latin words referring to plants, flowers, and gardening. As they stopped before a certain shrub and examined it, I wondered how much they could really see in the darkness.

Their wedding, two days later in Winchester Cathedral, was the spectacular event everyone expected it to be. For the short walk from the bishop's palace to the cathedral, I'd been chosen to carry the queen's ermine-trimmed train, so heavy that her chamberlain had to walk beside me and help. For the first time, my nearness to the throne was being publicly acknowledged. As the gates opened, we could hear the cheering of the crowds beyond, lining the street. Just before I stepped out onto the street behind the queen, I experienced a wave of fear so strong that I thought I would drop the train and barge my way back through the procession behind me. But I gripped the ermine with trembling hands and allowed it to lead me out. I kept my eyes fixed on the back of the queen's head, where her crown shone brilliantly, and steadily followed her into the midst of the applauding crowds on either side of the street. Slowly, the tension eased out of me, and halfway to the cathedral my excitement began to build. The queen had sent me a gown of white satin with silver thread for the occasion, and a new English hood trimmed with diamonds. Surely, some in the crowd must have noticed me, since for once I didn't just blend in with the other women in their identical gowns.

In the cathedral, I followed the queen down the red serge-draped causeway to where two thrones were placed in the choir, and where the king, dressed in a robe of rich brocade, and covered with diamonds and pearls, waited for her. With a feeling of great importance, I helped the chamberlain detach the train from the queen, and then took my seat off to the side as the ceremony began. Partway through, I would be required to receive the gold coins offered as a gift from the bridegroom, and my fears returned as the moment approached. But just as before, they vanished as I stepped forward with the queen's purse and received them. Fleetingly, her face turned toward me as I took them. I saw no fondness there, and wondered whether her newfound happiness would ever prompt her to allow me to marry.

Afterward, when the banquet and entertainments were over, and I was back in my cramped temporary rooms at the bishop's palace, I wrote to Father for the first time since receiving news of his marriage plans, so many months ago. I now felt I had no right to wish to see Father deprived of the same future I wanted for myself, though I would inherit none of his lands or titles. Today I had experienced a different heritage, the royal one I had received from my mother. If I continued to be careful, avoiding the pitfalls my cousins had not, it could put me in a strong position.

Of course, I didn't write to him of this, only of the day's festivities and my participation in them. At the end, I enquired politely as to his plans for his wedding. From this, he would understand that I had accepted it.

The following morning, the queen's women waited outside the bridal bedroom to see what clues her demeanour would give as to the success or failure of her wedding night. I hoped she'd been properly prepared, and at some time in her life had been told what to expect, as I had been. Mrs Brograve had explained matters to me very clearly some time before Sir Andrew had arrived at Brougham. "It's all very natural and easy and can be enjoyable, so long as no one makes too much fuss about it," she'd said. But for the queen, it would have been impossible to avoid a great fuss. Her hopes for the future depended on it. Also hovering outside the bedroom door was Bishop Gardiner and several other members of the council, waiting to receive the reddened bedsheet showing that the queen was no longer a virgin. Everyone knew the moment had particular significance, for the tragedy and suffering endured by the queen's mother had partly been caused by confusion over whether or not her first marriage to King Henry's older brother had been consummated.

After some time, the door opened and Mrs Clarencius stepped out. Holding the stained sheet like a banner for all to see, she proudly presented it to the bishop and councillors. Murmuring with approval, the bishop took it and led the councillors away.

Once they were gone, the women swarmed around Mrs Clarencius. "The king stayed nearly the entire night," she said triumphantly. "They have taken to each other in a way that is more than satisfactory for what is expected of them. But the queen is tired this morning and will need more time to get ready for Mass. She begs your pardon for this."

No sooner had we all seated ourselves again, when there was a commotion in the outer corridor, followed by a crowd of Spanish courtiers bursting into the room. From their boisterous talk and manner, it was evident they'd been up all night, and many of them appeared to have overindulged in wine. Mrs Clarencius rushed over to them, asking what they wanted, but they stared at her in confusion and replied in

Spanish. The only words I understood were "Queen Maria". Fortunately, there was an interpreter in the group, who was pushed to the front. He explained that in Spain it was customary for the court to greet the royal bride in her bed the following morning.

"You'll do no such thing," Mrs Clarencius said indignantly. "Her Majesty has had an exhausting night and doesn't need to be disturbed."

The interpreter looked surprised by her comment, but then tossed his hand helplessly and repeated what she'd said in Spanish. Loud laughter erupted from the group, but was instantly silenced by Mrs Clarencius angrily stamping her foot. The laughter stopped; the gentlemen in the group bowed, and they silently retreated from the room.

"Can you imagine the shock to the queen if I'd let that group in?" Mrs Clarencius murmured when they were gone. "It's time alone she needs now, to compose herself."

When the queen emerged from her seclusion a short while later, she not only looked sufficiently composed, but serenely happy. All the women gathered around her, but no one spoke. She then went to each of the women who had been married, her expression fondly knowing, and took each by the hand and kissed her cheek, a quiet statement that she was now one of their number. She then said, "Let us have our Mass," and led us to the chapel.

Over the following weeks it became clear that the queen had fallen deeply in love with the king. On the surface they seemed suited to each other, despite her greater age. However, on closer observation, discordances were apparent, which grew more striking the longer one watched them. Despite being smitten with her handsome husband, the queen seemed detached from him, as she did from everyone. He, for all his perfect manners and charm, began to appear artificial, as though he were a life-size handsome puppet, manipulated by someone unseen. His use of Latin with the English courtiers who knew it, or Spanish with the ones from his home — which almost no one at court understood — magnified his strangeness. It was as though we were all involved in a masque.

"It's like we're in some strange dream," Mrs Newton commented to me. "The Spanish courtiers look and sound so different from us. There are so many more people everywhere all the time, we're nearly stepping on each other."

"The king requires his own household," I offered.

With the exception of the young English noblemen selected as his closest attendants, the king clearly preferred his Spanish courtiers. But he did make an effort to ingratiate himself with the nobility, who liked him. While the queen was occupied with ruling the country, the king busied himself organising elaborate masques, games, dances, and hunting parties. As his popularity increased, so did the understanding that the queen could refuse him nothing, and powerful members of the nobility began to make their way to him.

17

The king's first appearance in London was set for a month after his arrival, following court visits to the palaces at Richmond and Windsor. Suffolk Palace, the splendid residence built and occupied by my grandparents, was conveniently located in Southwark near London Bridge, and was chosen for the overnight stay preceding the processional royal entry across the bridge into the city.

Despite the connection to my family, I felt no familiarity when we arrived at the beautiful and luxurious palace. I had been there but once, when my parents had brought me during our London visit shortly before my mother had died. I only remembered the isolated rooms on the third floor of the main section, where my uncle had lived and died. My unnerving encounter with the young Lord Darnley underscored this memory in an unsettling way as we arrived for our brief stay. Fortunately, the room assigned to me and Mrs Newton was in a completely different part of the palace.

Shortly after dinner, as I accompanied the other women outside to the gardens, I noticed whispers spreading among them. Knowing better than to enquire directly, I quietly asked Mrs Newton to find out what they were saying, telling her I suspected it was to do with my family connection to the palace.

In less than an hour, she found me in the solitary bower I had sought out. "It wasn't about the palace," she reported. "The Duchess of Northumberland visited the king this morning, accompanied by the Duchess of Alba. It's believed she has requested the king's help for the release of the Dudley men."

The duchess had been in seclusion since the execution of her husband, and then her son Guildford. But apparently she had overcome her grief sufficiently to attempt to help restore her surviving family.

Mrs Newton was adept at forming friendships at court, and had quickly got to know some of the new Spanish courtiers. She could already understand a bit of their language. She told me, "When the Duke of Alba saw there was nothing for his wife to do after the wedding, he took a house for her in Chelsea until the court goes to London. The Duchess of Northumberland lives nearby and called on her. If I'm understanding my Spanish friends correctly, the Duke and Duchess of Alba hold great influence with the king, which is why he saw her. They tell me the king already understood who the Dudleys are." She smiled knowingly. "He's a smart one, this king, for all his charm and game-playing and doting on the queen. He's no fool, and he appreciates the value of friendships. Even while the two duchesses were still with him, he said in Spanish to one of his attendants that the Dudleys are all men of ability, who could serve him well." She paused. "The attendant told my friend Sir Andrew's name was mentioned also."

"Did he say anything else about him?" I asked eagerly.

"He couldn't tell, because the king switched to Latin again to speak to the Duchess of Northumberland."

Our eyes met, but I knew we shouldn't speak of the possibility that had occurred to both of us. If Sir Andrew found the king's favour, he might seek to fulfil his previous marriage plans with me.

"Did your Spanish friends say how the king responded?"

"After the duchesses left, he was heard to say that he had an interest in the Dudley sons. But Sir Andrew was too old to be of use anymore."

Something inside me relaxed. My plans to marry Sir Andrew Dudley were firmly in the past.

The afternoon was fine, the gardens and orchards in full bloom. In the distance, the other women were laughing, playing some simple game. I wondered if my grandmother and her children had ever walked and played here, before their lives had been clouded by the struggle for the throne.

That evening, Mrs Clarencius told me the queen wanted to see me. I hurried to her rooms, immediately fearful that the summons had something to do with Sir Andrew Dudley.

The room was spacious, with elaborately carved woodwork, rich tapestries, and large windows. The king was present, playing with a pair of dice at a table off to one side. He observed me as I came in, his new scrutiny making it clear that he had never given me more than a passing thought, not even at his wedding. There had clearly been some discussion of me before I'd been sent for. He smiled, dipping his head slightly, then continued his game. The queen sat in the centre of the room, an empty chair beside her. I curtsied to them both.

The queen, who'd been gazing at her husband adoringly, looked at me. "Here already? You must have winged feet."

"Your Majesty asks so little of me, I am eager to comply with any requests."

She pointed to the empty chair, indicating that I should sit, which I did. She then said, "The king is quite taken with the beauty of this palace. I've been telling him the story of the Duke of Suffolk and his marriage to my aunt, which at first so distressed my father. But he finds the tale of love triumphant intriguing." She looked back at him, her eyes wide with fascination. Noticing he'd become the object of our attention, he smiled again, smoothly and serenely, showing he was well used to his wife's longing gazes. Then he shook the dice between his cupped hands and threw them out onto the table. His face showed that the result displeased him. Sighing with dissatisfaction, he leaned back in his chair.

The queen stood and went to him. She took his handsome face between her hands and kissed it, then smoothed his hair. Lovingly, she took the dice from his hands, shook them and tossed them. They both hovered over them intently as they rolled to a stop, then gave little cries of satisfaction. The king half rose from his chair and gave her a little bow, lifting an imaginary hat from his head and grandly waving it. He then seized her hand, pressed it to his lips, and released it. The queen turned and came back to me. Behind her, a look of mask-like blankness passed over the king's face, and he sat utterly still, an extreme contrast to the animation he had just displayed before the queen. Then, just as quickly, he grabbed up the dice to resume his solitary game.

The queen took her seat again, the skirt of her gown riding up just enough for me to see she had crossed her ankles girlishly. "The king was pleasantly surprised to learn there was another descendant of the great Duke of Suffolk and the lovely Mary Tudor. He thought the only ones were our unfortunate cousin Frances and her two daughters. He asked to meet you, and so here you are."

I saw that the king was observing me again; although the queen had spoken in English, he had followed her meaning. "Margaret … Clifford," he said slowly, pronouncing my name meticulously. Then, in very quick Latin, he asked if I had ever lived in the palace.

In Latin, I replied I had not, but that my mother had as a child. The queen then remarked that she had visited the palace often as a child, with her mother. To me, she said in English, "Those were happy times."

"I was thinking about my family's history here, this afternoon in the garden," I replied in English. I turned to the king, and in Latin told him my mother had loved Queen Catherine and had been chief mourner at her funeral. The mention of this pleased the queen. I then said that my mother and grandparents would have been delighted with the queen's marriage to a prince of Spain. In response, the king and queen looked at each other, and the king smiled fondly. I told them I had no doubt the union would be blessed.

Suddenly, for all its beauty, the palace felt heavy with the weight of my family's past. In Latin, I said I hated France and Scotland. Somehow, the angry words came more easily when spoken in a language I never used.

My change in tone surprised them, and both stared at me with interest. Emboldened, I wanted to say more — that the Scottish and the French had been responsible for the deaths of my uncles, brothers and mother. But I did not. Instead, still in Latin, I said that Scotland was the enemy of all who lived in the north. Satisfied, the queen's gaze shifted away from me, but the king's did not. The mask-like expression had returned to his face. In Latin, he asked if my dislike extended to my cousin the Queen of Scots; I answered that I didn't know her, but I distrusted her French and Scottish relatives. Gesturing to the room around us, I added that my grandmother had been unhappy during her short time as Queen of France. Her great love for my grandfather, I said, and her speedy marriage to him, had been prompted by a desire to return to England after being widowed.

The king didn't reply, but the mask remained in place; he was clearly analysing my response. I'd intended to convey the message that my grandmother's reluctance to be drawn into political schemes through marriage mirrored my own. I'd worked out that the real reason the king had wanted to see me was because he'd just heard of my involvement with Sir Andrew Dudley. He was still learning to navigate the court, appraising the various powers and factions of the nobility, and he now understood that I was possibly an important part of it. He would pass along this information to whoever his puppeteer was.

The mask was replaced by a smile, and he reached for the dice again. In Latin, he casually remarked that a few years ago there had been a plot to poison Mary Queen of Scots.

I was shocked; no one had made me aware of this. The king's comment also implied that he knew of the other deaths resulting from the struggle between my family and the Scottish royals.

Quickly, the queen said, "We won't detain you any longer, Lady Margaret. Thank you for spending this time with us."

Her voice was suddenly harsh. It was clear she didn't want the conversation to proceed in the direction the king had sent it. He heard her change in tone and looked at her, but then returned his attention to his dice. Once again, he cast them on the table.

I pretended to notice nothing. I stood up and said, "I am happy to find Your Majesties so harmonious."

The queen came as close to smiling at me as she ever did. "What news have you from your father?" she asked.

"He writes to me only of domestic matters." I hesitated. "He is preparing for his marriage to Lord Dacre's daughter."

"Yes," the queen replied simply. I curtsied and left.

As the door closed behind me, I knew I couldn't linger among the courtiers, with their idle conversation, shallow laughter and trivial games. The king's statement, and the queen's immediate termination of the conversation, had been yet another confirmation of what my father had told me of my family's tragedies. I'd known the queen had been aware of them — she'd spoken of them on the night we'd first arrived in London — but now I knew they were more widely known.

On the far side of the room, a woman laughed, and then others joined in. Next to them, a table of gentlemen were playing cards, and nearby another was starting to pluck the strings of some musical instrument. All around was conversation, some in English, some Spanish, but all of it lively and happy.

I made my way outside to the gardens and breathed in deeply. The air held the scent of the nearby Thames, which had flowed for centuries, indifferent to the countless people who had sailed or rowed upon it. And it seemed to me that it could be very dangerous indeed for those who never learned the currents.

The following afternoon, we entered the city in a long, formal procession. As we crossed London Bridge there was celebratory cannon fire, and all along the route to Whitehall Palace were elaborate pageants honouring the king. At the palace, wedding gifts awaited, including magnificent tapestries of gold and silver, a jewelled portable organ, and a tablet with a picture of the king and queen as parents to a long line of future English monarchs, waiting in the heavens to be born.

But despite the glory of the reception, there were signs that beyond the court the Spanish had not been entirely welcomed. Although the streets had been lined with cheering crowds, behind them I'd noticed citizens watching in silence, not overtly hostile but pointedly refraining from endorsing the welcome. At the palace, the servants stared at the Spanish suspiciously, and occasionally snickered and sneered. Once, from around a corner, I heard a group of footmen ridiculing Spanish speech, their imitations whiny, incoherent nonsense, which they all found hilarious. Mrs Newton whispered that there had been trouble between the Spanish and English servants, some of which had erupted into knife fights. She'd overheard remarks among the Spanish that they were afraid to leave the palace, fearing a similar reception on the city streets beyond the reach of the palace guards.

The stay in London was brief, and within days the court departed for Hampton Court. We were to remain there for the rest of the summer, the final phase of the king and queen's extended honeymoon.

Hampton Court proved to be the most comfortable of the royal residences, modern and well designed, with over forty apartments to accommodate the entire court. It was also prettier and less imposing than the other palaces, low and spreading and made of pink brick. In a noticeable position above the entrance to the inner gatehouse was an immense, almost fantastical clock, with separate dials showing not only the hours of the day, but the signs of the zodiac and phases of the moon. As we passed beneath it, it seemed an omen of the inevitable passage of time. For the queen, who was ageing, it was particularly significant, since she would only be capable of bearing children for a few more years.

The intimacy displayed by her and the king since their wedding had continued, with the king spending at least part of every night in her bedroom. An amused whisper had circulated among the women that Mrs Clarencius had been overheard saying the queen was always reluctant to let him leave her bed.

Physically, marriage suited the queen; she became heavier and less frail and pale. The king remained the same, ever polite and attentive, never appearing to resist his wife's incessant attentions. But his moments of studied stillness, when his face would go blank, became more frequent. Beneath his charming exterior there was clearly a great discipline.

When the king and queen were together, especially outdoors, the age difference between them showed. At times, it was impossible not to wonder how it was for him to kiss a woman who was already missing half her teeth. It was clear, though, that the queen would not wonder about this; she believed her marriage to be the work of God, a union that would be divinely maintained with little personal effort on her part. It was only at the insistence of her women that she continued to attend to her appearance, bathing more frequently than she was accustomed to, making use of perfumes in strategic places, and having her hair brushed. Mrs Clarencius attempted to make her understand that beautiful clothes and sparkling jewels were of no value to a woman's husband in the bedroom.

One day, while seated beside her husband on the dais in the Great Hall of Hampton Court, the queen passed wind loudly enough for those of us nearby to hear. For the first time, distaste showed on the king's face, and he leaned away from her, no doubt to escape the inevitable bad smell that would follow. But the lapse was momentary; very quickly his blank expression returned, followed by his usual smile of practised fondness.

Near the end of September, the queen suddenly appeared to be in a mood of unearthly joy, moving so lightly on her small feet that she appeared to be dancing. The king also looked different, more relaxed, as though some monumental task had been completed. The entire court was called together in the

Great Hall, and it was announced that the queen was with child.

Thunderous applause echoed through the hall. Overwhelmed, the queen turned and buried her face in the gold velvet sleeve of the king's coat. For once, genuine-looking satisfaction showed on his face, and he fondly patted the top of the queen's bonnet. Only those close enough could see how tightly the queen clutched his sleeve, as if she hoped the birth of their child would allow her to hold him forever. I looked away. The queen was married to an illusion; she had never seen the true man. The king understood his wife better, but fed her illusion in order to fulfil a task assigned to him by another — the puppeteer I now understood to be his father, the Habsburg Emperor Charles.

But whatever their true feelings were, the queen and king had conceived an heir. The queen's monthly flow had been missed, and all the other signs had been confirmed by the physicians. The child would be born in May.

18

As soon as we returned to London, a ball was held at Whitehall Palace in honour of the queen's condition. For the occasion the women dispensed with their usual livery and wore gowns of different hues, mine of light green. It was bold of me to choose one of the Tudor colours; I might not have done so a few months previously, for fear of appearing ambitious. But the queen's condition had altered the circumstances; her security on her throne was greatly increased, and less susceptible to challenges from rival claimants. Her wariness of me had seemed to relax after her betrothal to the king, and she had even chosen the other Tudor colour, white, for me to wear at her wedding.

Father had brought my jewels on his first visit, and I'd entrusted the case to Mrs Newton without even opening it. Before the ball, she brought it out for me, though I wasn't sure whether I'd wear any jewellery.

Opening the case, I was startled to find the golden eagle brooch Sir Andrew had given me. I had concealed it in my room before leaving Skipton, when Father had confiscated all his other gifts. Someone had found it — probably Mrs Brograve, from whom it had been notoriously difficult to keep any secrets — and put it with my other jewels, most of which had been my mother's. I picked it up and held it, as impressed as I had been the first time I'd seen it.

"A fine piece," said Mrs Newton, behind me. "Was it your mother's?"

"No," I answered. "But it could have been." I put it back and closed the case, deciding not to wear any jewels.

"Why?" asked Mrs Newton.

"That little brooch represents unreachable ambitions. I knew little of my mother, but I have come to understand she nurtured such aspirations."

"She was the youngest child?"

"The youngest of the two daughters from her father's first marriage. There was also one brother from that marriage who was younger than her."

"The boy would have been most important, and then the eldest sister," Mrs Newton said knowingly. "It's not fair, but it's just the way of it in any family, rich or poor. Sometimes the child who feels overlooked pushes the hardest to be seen when they grow up. It happened in my family. My youngest sister married a baron and strove tirelessly to accomplish it. He's an irate and rather ugly man. But she sits right beside him at the centre of the dais in their castle, and everyone sees her. She's not overlooked, not anymore."

What she'd just said might well have applied to my mother; her childhood had been different from mine. "I never felt overlooked as a child. For me it was the opposite — I was always the centre of attention. Shortly before I left the north, I'd begun to want more out of life, and the court sounded very exciting. Unfortunately, that desire was manipulated in a very dangerous way." I handed the jewellery case back to her. "And that is never going to happen again."

The queen was very much the centre of attention at the ball, wearing rich red velvet and numerous jewels, as usual. When the musicians began playing, the king led her out to the centre of the hall, where they could dance the pavane. The courtiers and guests immediately assembled in couples behind them, to begin the pattern of five intricate steps that would take them around the hall, lightly touching the fingers of their partners. All eyes were on the king and queen, and no one noticed when I quietly rose and slid into the shadows at the sides of the hall. If I'd stayed, some young gentleman would undoubtably seek me for his partner, and participating held no appeal for me. The artificiality of the queen's marriage disturbed me, as did my reminder earlier in the day of my involvement with Sir Andrew.

I made my way to a nearby door, and into the corridor beyond. I couldn't leave, as I would have liked to, since I needed to stay near enough to attend the queen. There was a stairway, which I knew led to the musicians' gallery, and a series of balconies perched around the hall. I could watch the dancing from one of these without being drawn into it.

Upstairs, through an open door I could see the musicians playing in their colourful outfits, and the music was loud. It softened as I walked down the long corridor that led to the balconies, all lit only by the torchlight from the hall. Some courtiers had found their way up to them, and were sitting or leaning on the railing, watching the dancing below. Finally, at the far end, I found one with no one present. Going to the edge, I looked over, enjoying the relief of finally being alone. Below, the dancers followed the king and queen around the hall, the colourful gowns and coats shifting.

"You have escaped also, I see, Lady Margaret," said a low, even voice nearby, startling me. A young man stepped out from the shadows at the other end of the balcony, where he'd been leaning against a pillar.

I recognised him as one of the seven young English noblemen who'd been chosen to attend the king: Henry Stanley, Lord Strange, son and heir of the Earl of Derby. The king favoured him, and he was the one who most often appeared with him, although he was the quietest and often had a look of sadness about him. The queen's women had decided that if not for his melancholy expression, he might well have been the handsomest of the king's gentlemen, either English or Spanish. He was tall, with blue eyes, a long face, a smallish nose and mouth, and curling, sandy-brown hair. His fairness contrasted favourably with the black livery usually worn by the king's gentlemen. Tonight, though, he wore fine garments of brown and yellow.

He started to introduce himself, but I stopped him. "I know who you are. Like me, you are the child of an earl, and like me, you are here to attend our sovereigns."

"But unlike me, you are part of the royal family," he said. "Although you don't act like it. I've seen you about the court. You don't behave as though you're anything more than one of the queen's women."

"I had an experience that taught me better."

"You refer to Sir Andrew Dudley?" He almost smiled, then said quietly, "I know Sir Andrew. We were both gentlemen of King Edward, before he died." He blinked and looked down at the dancers, but not quickly enough to conceal that the death of King Edward had been a blow to him, and that he still mourned him.

He was the first person I'd met who displayed genuine grief over the loss of my cousin. I remembered that a group of noblemen's sons of about the same age had been companions to him since childhood, educated alongside him at court. They must have been like siblings. "I didn't know King Edward, not at all," I said. "I met him but once. He was only a few months younger than me."

"I was six years older. He was like a younger brother to me."

"What was he like?"

The pavane music played in the distance while I waited for his reply. Eventually, he said, "He was happy and generous when his father was alive. But then came the deaths of all the adults around him, in the space of a few years: his father King Henry, his stepmother Queen Catherine Parr, his uncle Thomas Seymour, and then his uncle Edward Seymour. It was the last two that were the hardest for him. Something changed in him when they turned on each other, and then both died under the headsman's axe. The Dudley brothers tried to replace them, and the king responded to them positively. But it was never the same. They were greedy and ambitious, and they used him. He had retreated into religion, and they encouraged it. But they provided no real relief from the pressures and responsibilities he was facing, which could only have been terrifying for him." He paused. "Not only was he responsible for the mortal lives of his subjects, but his father had made himself head of the Church in England. So, he was responsible for his people's souls as well. I think in the end it was that which killed him, no matter what the actual illness was."

The portrait he was painting was horrifying. He had described the destruction of a young person who had been isolated and manipulated all his life. My life in the north, which I had started to dislike, had been idyllic compared to his.

The music from the gallery stopped, then started again, but faster. Down below, the king brought the queen to the throne and sat beside her. The rest of the court began another dance, the saltarello, less stately and formal than the pavane.

We both watched them for a while. I then asked, "But what of his sisters? Did they not visit him?"

His mouth tightened with disdain. "You know them," he said pointedly. "Each had her own concerns. They still do."

He'd already said more than he should have, which as a courtier he'd have known. For some reason, he found me trustworthy. It was clear he'd already observed me and decided I was someone who stepped carefully at court.

"Now, I attend this new king," he went on. "It's not the same. He's different, older than me by four years. But he is kind, and my melancholy troubles him. He sympathises with me because he has his own troubles." He gestured over the balcony. "How could he not, so married? But he says nothing of them."

Behind us, in the corridor, there were suddenly voices arguing, covered by the music but growing louder as they drew near. Some were English, some Spanish. Lord Strange immediately went to the quarrellers and ordered them to stop. "Even today, you must do this?" he said with disgust. "We celebrate one who will be both Spanish and English!"

They recognised him, and clearly knew he had the authority of close proximity to the king. Silently, they withdrew.

"They'll just start again outside," he said when he'd returned to me. "It will be years before this hostility ceases. It's even worse outside the palace, in the city."

"Surely the announcement that the queen is with child will help."

He shook his head. "It hasn't so far. It's mostly just the English fearing foreigners, but the Spanish often instigate trouble with their attitudes. No matter how polite they are, underneath they see us as barbarians and heretics. Before they arrived, all of them had heard how the queen's Spanish mother suffered here, and how the monasteries were stripped of their wealth. They think these are signs of a people without fear of God. The English can feel this from them, even without their saying it. It provokes them to be insulting in return, and they do their best to take advantage of the Spanish wherever they can. The Spanish get cheated and offered inferior goods and services throughout the city. The friars get the worst of it; they have been mugged, and stripped of their crucifixes and habits."

"I knew there was tension, but not so much."

"The queen believes God directed her choice of husband, and that her now being with child confirms it. If so, let us hope God will intervene to quell these disturbances. She will need his help." Strange looked back at the hallway, as though to make certain we were alone. Satisfied, he said, "She should have married Courtenay."

"You should be careful what you say," I replied with gentle disapproval.

"We are alone. And I know you will not repeat it."

"I won't. But why do you trust me?"

"You were clever enough to extricate yourself from the Dudley entanglement. Your cousins were not, and one of them is now dead. You are cautious."

"Edward Courtenay," I said pointedly, "is a fool. The queen is a good woman, and I would not wish her married to a fool."

Strange looked down at the crowd again, and then back at me, gesturing toward the two thrones where the royal couple sat. The queen reached over, holding the sleeve of the king's coat. "Only a fool," he said smoothly, "could tolerate *that*. And this king isn't one."

It was clear the queen believed her condition to be a sign of God's approval of her restoration of the old religion. So I wasn't surprised when we then began to hear that she was seeking to please God better — and ensure the birth of a healthy child — by pressing her Privy Council to agree to the return of lands taken from the Church during the reign of her father. Lord Strange, who had several times sought my company after our encounter at the queen's ball in October, told me the councillors had been vehement in their opposition. Despite his youth, he knew several of them, and they had spoken freely to him. "Even the most conservative of the lords benefitted from the dissolution of the monasteries," he said.

I thought of my family's extensive lands from the abbey of Bolton. "My family did also."

"As did mine. The councillors also feel that the queen is unappreciative of their having agreed to the Spanish marriage by now pressing for this. They told her they wouldn't approve her returning her own lands to the Church, either. The income, they said, was needed by the country, which would be impoverished by her actions. The queen was so angry she wept and stormed out of the meeting."

When we spoke, we were always in the large public rooms where we crossed paths, with others around, but we drew ourselves to one side for privacy. Even so, I was surprised when he replied to a remark I made about the queen's certainty of God's approval with a curt statement: "God is not of the old religion."

In a low voice, I asked, "You favour the Reformers?"

"No. I was educated as one, with King Edward. But I don't believe that the Reformist ways are any better or worse than the old religion."

I had never met an atheist, and now wondered if he could be one. My face must have shown my thoughts, for he laughed softly, which he seldom did. "No, I'm not an atheist. But I don't believe God cares much for the distinctions between the old religion and the new. It's mortals who engage in all of that, often using it to reflect their own troubles. I saw King Edward do it, and now Queen Mary." Darkly, he added, "It will get much worse now, with the queen. And I admit I fear that if King Edward had lived, he might have grown into a monstrosity of a Reformer."

"A terrible thing to suggest," I protested, but only because I felt obliged to; I agreed with much of what he said.

"I loved him. But something in him had become twisted and insecure, because of his losses and loneliness."

Two of the queen's women passed us. We stopped talking; he bowed to them, and I smiled. When they had moved away, he continued, "It will worsen now, with the queen, especially since she's been frustrated by her council. She's started to mention heresy. There will be difficult times ahead for those who don't believe as she does."

"Months ago, my father warned me there would be conflict over the Church lands. I agree there will be trouble, especially for those who are sincerely Reformers. I am fortunate, for like you, religion doesn't matter much to me one way or the other. My conscience isn't troubled by conforming either way."

"We are indeed fortunate in that," he agreed. "Also, our ambitions do not drive us to take advantage of the beliefs of others." He paused. "The Dudleys — and many others — used religion for their own benefit. But they had no convictions."

Strange's remark about the Dudleys stayed with me. A few days later, when we spoke again, I said, "Tell me of Sir Andrew Dudley."

It was afternoon, and we were with the court in the gardens of Whitehall, following the king and queen in the fragrant autumn air. For all her obsession with the king, the queen still diligently devoted most of each day to the work of running her kingdom, spending long hours with her councillors and the many petitioners for her attention and favour. The marriage agreement excluded the king from participation in the government. But whenever he pressed the queen for something, nominally for the sake of her health and that of their child, he was usually successful, as he had been this afternoon in drawing her away from the council.

"I've heard Sir Andrew is to be pardoned," Strange said. "His nephews have already been released. But Sir Andrew was a little more deeply involved in the plotting, and his release will take more time."

"By 'more deeply involved', you mean his planned marriage to me."

"Yes."

We continued along the path slowly, at the very rear, creating a distance between us and the others. "Was that truly the king's choice? I know all about his devise for the succession, and his concern with leaving a male heir of Tudor lineage. But did that start with the king, or was it suggested by the Dudleys?"

"It was the king; he wished to ensure his religious legacy would continue after he died." Strange spoke with the certainty of one who'd been present at the time. "Northumberland manipulated that desire to his advantage. His brother helped. The king liked both of them, and he listened to them. They knew he saw in them the reflection of his uncles who'd died — on his orders."

"Sir Andrew was the same as his brother?"

"Yes and no. He was more of a soldier, less polished, and the king responded to the adventurous aspects of his life, all his talk of fighting the Scots and the French. It was different from the lives the rest of his attendants had lived. But Sir Andrew wasn't just a good storyteller. He was calculating, and skilled at managing the king's wardrobe and jewels. There, he was different from the duke: he had a penchant for beautiful things of value. His house in London was full of all sorts of luxuries. He wasn't as rich as the rest of us, who had family fortunes. The king saw this and frequently gifted him with jewels, taking great satisfaction in seeing his gratitude."

"He sent many precious and valuable things to Skipton when we were to be married."

"You were another. The king was making him a gift of the wealthiest heiress in England, with a claim to the throne."

I stopped walking and stared straight ahead. The remark was rude and diminishing. "What an ugly thing to say," I said frostily.

To my annoyance, he gave a dismissive laugh. "Oh, come now, don't be angry." I said nothing, and the look on his face changed, showing he knew he'd made a mistake but didn't know how to retreat from it. As the son of one of the most important earls in the kingdom, apologising wasn't something he'd be familiar with. "Well, don't blame me just for saying it," he said eventually. "Blame your father for accepting Sir Andrew as a suitor for you."

"You are mistaken," I said in as condescending a tone as I could manage. "My father did not accept Sir Andrew's marriage proposal. I did. It was the mistake of a sheltered and foolish young woman, but I am no longer such, and I do not like being mocked for what I once was. And, to inform you correctly, I will shortly no longer be the wealthiest heiress in England. My father is soon to remarry and will no doubt have a son to inherit his titles and estates."

"You'll still get all the money and property the Duke of Suffolk left your mother, and you have a claim to the throne," he said bluntly.

"And there will still be many who see me as a great prize to be won," I said. "But for all your sneering amusement, does it not occur to you that your position is much the same?" I laughed so loudly and harshly that up ahead on the path, several courtiers turned and looked back at us. "What a prize the heir to a valuable earldom would be, and one that has always been close to the Tudor throne! Do not think to reproach me for my choices in accepting King Edward's altering the succession. If I remember correctly, your father the Earl of Derby swore to uphold that change. Did not you also sign the document yourself, as one of the king's gentlemen?"

His blue eyes widened, and he inhaled sharply. "I sought to follow the wishes of a dying king," he said defensively.

"So did I. Most of us did. He was the king, wasn't he? No matter how he'd been manipulated, the requests — orders — came from him. If anyone is to be blamed, it should be those around him who never tried to make him see the self-serving motives of those influencing him. Tell me, Lord Strange, did you try?"

He looked away from me. "It was impossible," he said, his voice so low it was almost a whisper.

His grief had been touched, and for all my agitation, I regretted my words. Of course, he would be bitter at the Dudleys for their part in the king's destruction, a bitterness that had been briefly directed at me for my association with them. "Yes, I see that it would have been hard," I said. "But I thought that might have taught you to sympathise with the difficulties of one in my position."

Before he could reply, I turned and went back to the palace.

19

For a while after that, Lord Strange and I avoided each other, and if we couldn't, we offered nothing more than the politest bow or curtsey of acknowledgement as we passed.

"What happened?" asked the observant Mrs Newton. "Did you quarrel?"

I could have told her but chose not to. Not because of the unkind things we'd said to each other, but because I didn't want her to see that I missed his conversation. Not only had he spoken engagingly — once he exerted himself past his subdued and withdrawn demeanour — but he'd told me much of what he knew about the doings of the Privy Council. Without that news, I was forced to rely on my own limited observations.

One thing that was increasingly apparent was the amount of time the queen spent with the friars who had arrived from Spain with the king. After meeting with them, people noticed her conversation tended to be full of talk of heresy, the stronger enforcement of religious conformity, and her responsibilities to God who had so blessed her. The priests spoke of it also, from the altar at our daily Masses, in increasingly dark and strident tones. Punishment was frequently mentioned, as a deterrent for those who might think to stray from what the priests and friars, and the queen, thought to be the one true religion. All of the Reformers had long ago left the Privy Council, and the few who had occasionally continued to appear at court had stopped. Some had fled the country entirely, going to Germany or Switzerland. Now, even those who conformed but favoured a moderate attitude toward the Reformers began to absent themselves from court. Others, whether long adherents to the old religion or recently returned to it, began to appear more frequently at the Masses held several times a day at court, and more gold crosses appeared as part of their attire.

There was also a very noticeable increase in King Philip's social activities, as though he was seeking an outlet for the frustrations of his powerless position. They moved away from table games and graceful dances to combat-focused entertainments. There were masques with militant themes, and jousts and tournaments, held with great fanfare. Participants wore colourful costumes and armour, although staffs and canes were used instead of lances.

In one of them, shortly after Parliament opened in November, Lord Strange participated prominently. He had clearly applied himself to learning the Spanish *juego de cañas*. He equalled the proficient Spanish gentlemen in skill, and he won. One of his prizes was a wreath of flowers presented to him by the queen, for him to give to one of her attendants or noblewoman guests. To my surprise, he strode directly to where I sat in the stands with the queen's women and, kneeling, offered it to me.

There was the sound of trumpets and applause all around the large courtyard. The attention of the crowd was so sudden I hadn't time to be unnerved by it. I rose and took the wreath from him with a steady hand, even managing to utter some ridiculous remark of gratitude. Our eyes met as I did, and I understood it to be his apology for his rudeness of several weeks ago. I hoped the amused expression on my face would equal his own.

When we were leaving, the king and queen passed close by me. Halfway through my usual curtsey of respect, I saw they had stopped. The king was looking at me. "Margaret ...

Clifford," he said, his tone mildly curious. Beside him, the queen looked at me with no particular interest.

An idea sprang to mind, and I acted on it, addressing the queen. "Your Majesty, this wreath should go to you, as the first of women among us." I held it out to her.

One of the interpreters stepped forward and quickly repeated my words in Spanish for the king. The queen stared dully at the offered wreath but didn't take it. "He gave it to you," she said vaguely.

"Then let me offer it to you in honour of your expectations, and to acknowledge the hopes of all here today for a little prince."

This time, her attention was captured, as I'd expected it would be. Her eyes widened with appreciation, and she looked very pleased as she nearly snatched the wreath from my hands. "Thank you, Lady Margaret. Surely God will bless us with the fulfilment of your wish."

Beside her, the interpreter again rapidly translated for the king. I'd used his method of mentioning the child to motivate the queen, and a quick look of sharp understanding flickered across his face before the blank mask returned. Then, they both moved on, the queen clutching the wreath.

The following morning, as I prepared to join the other women to accompany the queen to Mass, she sent a message that she wanted to speak to me. I found her in bed, just finishing her morning consultation with her leading doctor, who was apparently well satisfied with her condition. "The child should quicken in about a month from now," he was saying. He peered down at her. "Do you understand? You will feel the child move."

"I thought I felt him do so last month," she replied.

The doctor shook his head. "Too early," he said.

"If God wills it, it is possible," the queen countered. "In the Old Testament, Sarah, the wife of Abraham, conceived when past the age a woman does."

The doctor bowed and said nothing else. On his way out, he told Mrs Clarencius to watch for signs of the quickening. "And do not mistake it for wind," I heard him say quietly as they passed.

The queen was sitting up in bed, swathed in a large blue robe, beneath which her distended stomach was visible. She was gazing straight ahead, lost in her thoughts, one hand resting protectively on her stomach. Her face showed an odd combination of tension and tranquillity.

"Your Majesty wished to see me?" I said as I approached.

Startled, her head jerked toward me. "Yes," she said. She waved her hand, indicating that I should stand directly beside her bed. I drew closer. The heavy crimson bed hangings and covers seemed overwhelming, like a huge trap in which the queen had been caught.

Close up, and without her rich garments and jewels, she looked different than she usually did, her dark red hair now appearing a muddy brown. It looked thin, and trailed lifelessly on her shoulders. Her face was extremely pale, and there were shadows beneath her blue eyes.

"Thank you again for the wreath yesterday," she said. "But it was given to you. You should have kept it." Her voice was as deep as ever, but so toneless she could have been thanking me for opening a door.

"It suited Your Majesty better than me," I said.

"The king thinks you would be well matched with Lord Strange."

The crimson bed canopy and hangings seemed to sway. "Matched?" I whispered.

"Married," she said decisively. "Are you agreeable? If so, I will write to your father, suggesting it. There are advantages, and it would be an appropriate match for you." Unexpectedly, one of her hands sprang out and seized one of mine. "Do you like him?" she asked urgently. "Do you love him, or think you can? If you do, he will love you in return." She leaned forward and stared directly into my face, as though desperate to see the truth of whatever I felt.

It was all I could do to refrain from pulling my hand back. Somehow, I managed to ask, "Must I decide right now?"

She released my hand and leaned back on the pillows. "Certainly not. But will you consider it? The king has already spoken to Lord Strange, and he is agreeable. The next step is for me to write to his father as well as yours, to find out if a satisfactory agreement can be reached." She waved her hand dismissively. "Mere trifles. Both earls will be satisfied with the proposal, I have no doubt. You and Lord Strange are well suited in station, fortune, and education. But I will not press you if you do not like him." She grimaced. "There were those who pressed me to marry Edward Courtenay. I knew such a marriage would never succeed." Both of her hands returned to her stomach.

I remembered my fears that she would never let me marry and conceive a child, which could threaten her throne. Now, since she was about to produce an heir, she felt secure enough to no longer see me as a threat. I now had an opportunity to move forward and make a life of my own. "Your Majesty is kind and generous to have such concern for me," I said. "But I need time to be sure of my decision. Once before I didn't fully understand matters regarding a marriage. You must forgive me if I seem overly cautious. I am anxious to avoid another mistake."

"Lord Strange is no Sir Andrew Dudley," she said scornfully. "This is a suitor worthy of you. Your caution speaks well of you, Lady Margaret, and I am pleased to see it. I see the match does not displease you. Are you agreeable to considering it?"

"Yes, Your Majesty," I replied, with difficulty.

She folded her hands together. "Very well, then. I will write to both earls, and have the king inform Lord Strange of how matters stand. Advent is upon us, and then the Christmas season. I suggest that you spend some time in Lord Strange's company. After the festivities, you may well know your mind."

Mrs Newton was sitting beside the ceramic stove with her sewing when I returned to my rooms. She looked at me in alarm. "Are you well? You've gone quite pale."

I started to answer, but no words would come. I stood uncertainly in the centre of the outer room, unable to bring myself to tell her what the queen had just said to me, as though doing so would represent a commitment to the marriage on my part. An instant later, I burst into tears. Covering my face with my hands, I ran into my bedroom and threw myself down on the bed. Fear took hold of me, all the more powerful because I didn't understand why I felt it. What I had hoped for since arriving at court — the queen's willingness for me to marry — had now been achieved. But instead of happiness and relief, I felt agitation and dread.

I heard light footsteps: Mrs Newton had followed me in. She placed a blanket over me, and I grasped the silk border and pulled it close around me. The side of the bed sank down as she sat on it. She didn't question me, but simply waited.

It was some time before I was able to say, "A marriage between me and Lord Strange has been proposed by the queen. The king suggested it."

"You have just now learned of it?"

"The queen asked if I was agreeable. I told her I needed time to consider it."

"Of course." She paused. "I thought that might have been the reason you and Lord Strange fell out with each other. I thought you might have refused him."

I lifted my head and turned to look at her. "You were thinking that even back then? This doesn't surprise you?"

"It seemed clear it would develop so. The match would be suitable for both of you. Several of the other women have said as much, too."

I sat up, pulling the blanket up to my shoulders. She got up and brought me a handkerchief, and I wiped the tears from my face. After she'd seated herself on the bed again, she said, "I'd have thought you would be happy. Lord Strange is handsome and affable, one of the most eligible unmarried men in the kingdom. The king himself favours the marriage. What is it that troubles you?"

"Another king favoured another marriage for me, once," I said. The cause of my fear began to take shape. "It nearly led to my destruction. My cousin Jane is dead, because of hers. Is it any wonder I should respond so?"

Her answer was quick. "Lady Jane died because of her father's treason. It's well known the queen meant to treat her and her husband with lenience, until the Duke of Suffolk revolted. You too would have suffered but a mild fate had your marriage with Sir Andrew Dudley come about. It wasn't the marriage, but the foolish judgement and politics of those around Lady Jane that brought her to the executioner's block. Your father doesn't meddle in such things, as hers did. Lord Strange is far from reckless: he is prudent and cautious. And you, Lady Margaret, have your own wisdom and understanding, from your months at court. No, you need have no fear of marriage bringing about your destruction."

I felt the truth of her words, and my fear receded somewhat. But there were other concerns. "Lord Strange has moods, and his melancholy sometimes seems deliberate, a method of getting his way with others," I said. "His conversation and agility of mind please me, it is true. But marriage to such a man would not be easy. And I do not love him."

"Would you imitate the queen's great love for the king?" Mrs Newton challenged. The delicacy of her tone and the look on her face told me that she understood the self-delusion the queen was indulging in. I had not previously known the extent to which it was ridiculed by everyone at court. The queen believed her obsession to be love, but in truth it had little to do with its recipient.

"There are things more important than romantic love," Mrs Newton continued. "I've learned that myself, and I think it's an even more important lesson for someone in your position. You want a life of your own, don't you? You want children and a household, with hundreds of people looking to you to lead them? It's what a woman like you was born to do — to use your power and influence to shape the lives of others. Or do you wish to live alone forever here, in the shadow of the queen?"

For a long while I silently lay on my bed, still holding the blanket over me. Then I pushed it off and got up.

"Your bonnet is sideways," she told me, and I reached up and put it right. Then I smoothed down the skirt of my dress, which fortunately hadn't been too badly crumpled. The queen was unlikely to join the women for Mass, but I would still be expected to appear, and I would now have to hurry to join them on time.

During the Mass, as I listened to the daily prayer for the safe delivery of the queen, I decided there was no need to hurry to accept Lord Strange. The queen's being with child had changed her attitude toward me. I had time, and I was not going to make another mistake.

At dinner Lord Strange was in his usual place with the king's gentlemen. Seeing him, even from a distance, I felt awkward and shy, which I rarely felt around anyone, least of all someone well known to me. But the way in which I knew him had shifted dramatically. Intimacy between us would be a part of our marriage, and to know that a man found me agreeable in that way was unusual for me. Sir Andrew had indicated he found me so, but that hadn't been the same. We had been in the north, in the quiet and relaxed surroundings of my family castles. Here, I was in the midst of the ever-watchful eyes of the court, where one's life easily became the subject of talk. The queen's marriage had been minutely observed and discussed, and, as her kinswoman, mine would also be.

After dinner, Lord Strange approached me. "The king and queen would see us married," he said quietly, as we followed them from the hall. His demeanour was smooth and unruffled; apparently his concerns didn't match my own. His confidence was both irritating and appealing.

"So I am told," I answered politely, striving for a touch of indifference.

"Your father will find me an acceptable suitor, no doubt?"

"My father's decisions are steeped in wisdom."

"He will consult the stars," he replied. Apparently, Father's study of astrology was well known.

"The stars do not compel. We have our will to decide. But they were created by God to advise us, and we are wise to make use of them."

"You are a scholar, I believe."

"I'm not — not in the way of the Lady Elizabeth, or the unfortunate Lady Jane. I haven't the inclination to spend so much time reading. Besides, there are other lessons to be learned in life, ones that do not come from books."

"Ones you have learned well." He looked at me meaningfully. "Much better than Lady Jane did, or Lady Elizabeth. Where are they, and where are you?"

"And you, Lord Strange, have smoothly shifted from serving one king to serving another, despite such altered circumstances. You too, it would seem, have knowledge that was not gained from books."

Pleased, this time he smiled as he said, "But not as quickly learned, or as thoroughly."

We were passing through one of the many large rooms on the way back to the queen's quarters, where the king typically stayed with her for a time after dinner, before she returned to work with her council. Lord Strange gestured to one side and we both stepped away, allowing the others to pass on without us. At the tail end of the line came a little group of friars, silent as always.

When the friars had passed, he rested back against a tapestry-covered wall, and said, "It's going to get worse, with them. The queen is attentive to their insistence on conformity in religion. They're Spaniards, but even the king doesn't approve of the extremity of their attitudes, and their influence on his wife. The queen feels she must do everything she can to thank God for rewarding her with a child. She knows now that she isn't going to succeed in returning monastery property to the Church, and she may seek another way of thanking God. I fear it may be a type of gratitude that reflects her anger at the nobility's refusal to give up their property, and the people's continued rejection of the Spanish. We may soon see a very dark time in this land." He gazed at me meaningfully. "It might be preferable to have a retreat from the court. Being established in one's own household would have advantages. My father has told me he intends to present me with several estates when I marry." He was telling me we would have our independence, if married.

"It would be fortunate to have a place to get away to, for many reasons," I said. "The boredom here at court becomes insufferable at times. While I was still in the north, I imagined it to be a place of constant excitement. But the queen's only real interests seem to be music, cards, and the king, And religion, of course."

"And ruling her kingdom."

"Certainly, that too. But we don't share in any of that, except the music and cards, which isn't very satisfying. There's not much for us to do here. I don't remember how my days were occupied before I came here. There were my lessons from my tutor, but I can't remember much of what we did in the evenings."

"You didn't play cards? Or any other games?"

"Not often. My father preferred to spend his time alone with his books."

"I expect you would be quite good at cards. We must play. I'd be happy to show you the newest games."

He beckoned one of the attendants hovering near the doors, and told him to bring cards to the queen's anteroom.

There, we found a little table off to the side, and when the cards were delivered, Lord Strange proceeded to show me a game he had recently learned from one of the Spanish gentlemen. His mood became more jovial as he did, and he laughed easily, pleased that I learned so quickly. We played for a while, during which he won almost every time, but then our winnings became more evenly divided. I began to excel, and when I had won several games in a row, he no longer laughed so easily, and his face took on a sour look.

After I'd won for the fifth time in a row, he threw down his cards. "Enough of this," he said. "It becomes such a bore after a while."

I leaned back in my chair. "You don't really resent my winning, do you?" I asked.

"Resent it?" he asked with exaggerated surprise. "Why ever would I resent it? I am pleased you learned so well." It was clear he was now uncomfortable that his irritation had been so visible.

"If I have done well, it is only due to the excellence of my teacher," I said. "Thank you, Lord Strange, for having taken the time."

His mood shifted abruptly, his confidence and poise returning. "The time has been well spent, Lady Margaret."

We got up and went in search of the rest of the court.

20

With the arrival of the Advent season, the court activities became much more subdued and infrequent, and it was a relief to have Lord Strange to talk to again. But I avoided playing cards with him, especially after I had the opportunity to surreptitiously watch him playing with another gentleman. Lord Strange lost, several times in a row; he was not, after all, a good card player. But his response was one of good-natured indifference, without a trace of the resentment he'd shown when he'd lost to me.

He was also vaguely disdainful when he spoke of the queen, and the king's subservience to her. His remarks were careful, but it was clear that he felt the king's judgement was superior, despite his being a foreigner unfamiliar with the ways of England. If I chose to defend the queen's political judgement — for she had survived extreme hardship and brought herself to the throne — he was dismissive. But there was often something about the way he responded that didn't feel authentic, as though he knew he was wrong but wouldn't admit it. At times, it seemed he simply disliked a woman having so much power.

It was that, more than anything else, that continued to deter me from agreeing to the marriage. Although we were in many ways equal, in the end, I was part of the royal family and he was not. It was a difference that would always lie between us and cause tension in our marriage.

Father's approval had come swiftly, as had the Earl of Derby's, and the outline of the marriage settlement had been easily agreed upon. Father had written that he had even once considered Lord Strange as a potential husband for me, should we have proved compatible with each other:

His family has long been associated with the Tudors. Your great-great-grandmother Margaret's last husband was of that family, and they helped bring Henry Tudor to the throne. Their wealth is vast, and their home, Lathom House, rivals any of the royal palaces. If you like each other sufficiently, you could not be better matched. Your children will draw an excellent lineage from both parents.

New fears began to creep into my mind at the thought of those children. They would have an important place in the succession, after the queen's children. They would be untouched by questions of illegitimacy, or a parent's treason, and would not have been excluded from the succession by either King Henry or King Edward. To be so positioned could be dangerous; I remembered the fate of my mother, brothers and uncles, as well as the measures taken to prevent the poisoning of my little cousin Lord Darnley. I wondered if my marriage to a less powerful husband and having children without so rich and influential a father would seem less of a threat to those with ambitions. But to choose to live so would be a betrayal of who I was, and of those who had come before me. That was something I could not reconcile myself with.

The Advent season, a time to await the celebration of the birth of Jesus, was a continuous reminder of the importance children would play in my future. I had little doubt that it held the same significance for the queen. Her joy lasted throughout Advent, Christmas Day and the week of festivities that followed. But on the day after New Year's, she became ill. She had caught a cold, which had been aggravated by her overexertion during the gift-giving ceremonies of the previous day.

Her usual doctors were summoned, along with two new ones. It was announced that the illness was not serious, but enough to keep the queen in bed, resting; the festivities were to be presided over by the king alone. The merriment resumed, with much laughter and chatter, both in English and Spanish. But a few days later, I began to notice that Mrs Clarencius was noticeably subdued. She had been kind to me, and although I did my best not to allow myself to be drawn into problems at court, seeing her so troubled me. "Are you well?" I finally asked her. "I've noticed you seem unsettled of late."

She looked as though she had just woken from a dream. "No," she said vaguely, but then she focused and quickly corrected herself. "I mean, yes, I am fine. Thank you for asking. Everyone else here is so selfish they never notice anything." She hurried away, leaving me convinced that something was indeed wrong. I therefore wasn't too surprised when on the afternoon of the day before the Epiphany, a short while before supper, she came to my rooms.

She was agitated and extremely pale, with shadows beneath her eyes. Discarding her usual polite tone, she brusquely told Mrs Newton to leave us. "Wait at the end of the corridor," she said. "If anyone comes and tries to linger near this door, send them away. Use any excuse you want — just get them away from here. What I have to tell Lady Margaret isn't for eavesdroppers."

Wordlessly, Mrs Newton got up and left. "Please sit down," I urged Mrs Clarencius, gently leading her to a chair. "I have some wine here."

She refused the wine and sat very stiffly, staring straight ahead. "Sweet Jesus help us all," she whispered. Her eyes darted around the room; she was uncertain how to begin. I sat down across from her, sympathetic to her distress.

Gripping her hands together, she finally managed to say, "I think the queen is mistaken about being with child." She sobbed and lifted her clenched hands before her as though in prayer.

My first thought was that she had taken leave of her senses; the queen's condition was well established. "But how could that be?" I asked gently. "She shows all the signs of it. Everyone has seen them. And her doctors have confirmed it."

She closed her eyes and shook her head. "I thought so at first, along with everyone else. Her monthly flow had ceased, and then her body began to expand in the expected places. I've never had children, but I've seen many of the court women carry them, and I've helped with all the stages along the way. I know what should happen. But from the very first, there were things that were different. The queen showed none of the changes of appetite, or distress in the mornings, that I have seen every other time. I discounted it and thought it a sign of God's favour toward her. But then the child never quickened as it should have. She believes it did, but I think that she just had wind, which she has always suffered from. There are other things, too — she moves and sits differently from every woman I've ever seen carrying a child."

As she spoke, my incredulity faded. "But what of the doctors?" I managed to ask.

"Oh, what do they know?" she said scornfully. "They see her only for a short time each day, and she barely lets them touch her! I am with her all the time!" She made a fist and struck her palm. "Now, finally, someone else has seen it as I have. A new doctor came to her, a Neapolitan who followed the Spanish here. He's done well in London because he lets it be known that he's Italian, not Spanish, and many rich London merchants have been finding their way to him. He was brought in to decide the proper herbs for the queen when she took ill. Afterward, he drew me aside to question me, and I could tell by what he asked that he thought as I did — that there is no child. He told me he has seen this before: when a woman so desperately wants a child, her body changes as if she had one. But there is nothing there."

"But what did the others say when he told them?" I asked.

"He didn't. He was afraid. He told only me, because he saw that I already knew. But he has now left the country, fearful that there will be consequences for those attending the queen when it is finally acknowledged."

"Perhaps he is wrong —"

"No. I then spoke with midwives I know. The oldest of them know of the condition he speaks of. They say it will not be understood until the due date passes with no child. Then there will be recalculations of the time of conception, and further months of desperate hope. Finally, after the woman accepts that there is no child within her, her body will return to normal."

A silence followed. Exhausted, Mrs Clarencius leaned back in her chair. What she had just told me was shocking and scarcely believable. But somehow, I knew it was true; it fit perfectly with the self-delusion that had surrounded the queen's marriage from the very first appearance of the king's portrait. And all my life, I had overheard remarks from gentlewomen and servants alike that it was the midwives and old women who were to be trusted in such matters.

"I can't tell her," Mrs Clarencius said. She looked at me imploringly. "I came here to ask if you can."

"No."

"You are her closest relative! Who other than you can be trusted with such dreadful news?"

It was impossible to imagine how such a conversation could take place. "She wouldn't believe it," I said. "Not from me, or you, or both of us together. The queen believes her conception is the work of God. She will invoke him to reject any doubts you raise. I think it is something she will have to understand herself, little by little. The shock of being forced to face it all at once might be too much for her."

"It could kill her," she said, frightened. "Or destroy her mind."

"The queen is strong, no matter her delusions. Her life has been full of disappointments. But she keeps her own counsel — and God's. So this is one thing we must wait for her to understand and accept on her own." I stood up. "You must decide for yourself what to do. But this is what I believe. I will not tell her."

Mrs Clarencius breathed deeply, and as she exhaled her tension appeared to ease. She would do as I did — say nothing — and she was relieved that the awful responsibility had passed her by.

I saw that she had aged considerably over the past few days. The strain of her knowledge, and her uncertainty of how to proceed, had been almost more than she could bear. Serving the queen had been her life, and she was devoted to her wellbeing, which stood poised to be shattered. All of Europe had been told of the expected child, and both she and the king would appear great fools. The king would likely leave; it was already believed that he would stay in England only until the birth of his child, before moving on to fight in the Spanish wars in Europe.

The queen would be distraught, angry and frightened, fearful that God had deserted her, or that she had failed to satisfy him. There was no telling what the effect would be on her already pronounced desire for religious conformity. Once again, she would begin to fear those with claims to her throne, especially those who could have a child. It could affect me, and her willingness for me to marry might change.

Mrs Clarencius stood up slowly, like a very old woman. "I will not tell her either," she said heavily.

I stood and moved toward her. "We should tell no one we have spoken of this. There will be great turmoil when it is finally known. Some will seek scapegoats, and the queen might be so troubled she could become confused as to who her true friends are. The Neapolitan doctor, I think, was wise to go abroad."

Mrs Clarencius didn't reply, but I could see she agreed. She'd been with the queen for so long that she well understood the volatility of the court, and the need to avoid the inevitable chaos that would ensue over the next few months. She took a step toward the door. "I am so tired," she said. "I must sleep for a while now. But after that, the queen will need me."

She went out. Mrs Newton returned and looked at me questioningly, but I held up my hand. "No, this I cannot speak of, even to you." She refrained from asking anything else, but must have sensed that I was about to say more, for she stood quietly, waiting. After a moment, I told her I had decided to marry Lord Strange. "I will tell him tonight," I said.

The barest trace of surprise showed on her face, and then she half-smiled. She understood something had happened that had helped me make up my mind.

"Any man in this kingdom worthy enough for me to marry will dislike my having greater power, because of my birth," I said. "Sir Andrew Dudley appeared not to, but I wasn't with him for long enough to see if it were truly so. And his greater age likely made him feel he had an advantage over me. It is true that Lord Strange shows signs of an ill temperament, and the marriage will not be an easy one. But I believe children can be an equaliser between us. If not, I will contend with it; but I know now that I could expect much the same of any lord that I marry. I do like Lord Strange, and I don't want to wait any longer. I wish for the wedding to take place as soon as possible."

The date was set for early February. The wedding was to be held in the chapel at Whitehall Palace, followed by a magnificent banquet. Everyone was pleased by my decision: Lord Strange, when I told him, leaned forward and kissed me. The next day, he gave me a spectacular ring of pearls and diamonds, which fit my finger perfectly. The queen sent me a jewel also, a brooch of diamonds, which I vaguely remembered having seen among the gifts Sir Andrew had sent to Skipton. She also decided I could dispense with her livery of black and russet, and wear what I liked. To facilitate my doing so, she sent me bolts of fine velvet, brocade and satin for new dresses, and for my wedding dress, tissue of gold and silver. Again, it all had a familiar look to it, very similar to what had previously been sent to Skipton for my wedding there. And when the queen sent me a message that she would give me all the plate and linens I would need for my household as a wedding gift, I knew without asking that they had been part of Sir Andrew's property that Father had turned over to her.

In late January, I was walking along a palace corridor, when ahead of me the guards opened a door and a man emerged, who struck me as someone I knew.

It was Sir Andrew Dudley. Startled, I drew back against the wall.

He proceeded down the corridor and passed without noticing me. He had aged terribly; the tragic events of the past two years having taken their toll upon him. The confident stance of the successful soldier and courtier was gone, and instead there was a stoop to his shoulders. He walked slowly, with his head bowed. As he passed, I saw deep lines and creases that had not previously marked his face. He had the look of a man who had been defeated by life.

I watched as he receded down the corridor, and then vanished around a corner. He had survived his troubles; his presence in the palace spoke of it. His sister-in-law, the Duchess of Northumberland, had worked well on behalf of her family. All the surviving Dudley men had finally been released, and it was said that the king wished to rehabilitate all of them into his service. Sir Andrew's release had come last, and I now understood it had been linked to my imminent marriage to Lord Strange. The queen's suspicions over the depth of my commitment to him had lingered until she had seen my willingness to marry another.

I stayed where I was for a while, to be sure that Sir Andrew was gone. Other courtiers passed, some laughing and chatting, others silently hurrying about their business, but no one took any notice of where I stood. Then, I went to find Lord Strange, who I now called Henry.

The remaining days before my wedding passed more quickly than I'd have believed possible, with all the preparations. I ended each day with relief that the inevitable announcement of the queen's disappointment had still not happened. I did not want her to have time to stop my wedding. It was not until the night before that I allowed myself to believe it was truly imminent.

All the queen's women had finally left my rooms, and I was left alone with Mrs Newton. I was looking at a tiara of silver and diamonds, a wedding present my father had given me earlier in the day.

"A beautiful gift," said Mrs Newton, behind me.

"It was my mother's. My father gave it to her in the early, happy days of their marriage."

I held it up, and she leaned in to look at it more closely. "Will you wear it tomorrow? No doubt your father would be pleased if you did."

"I am trying to decide." She stepped away, and I set it down on the table before me. After a while, I rewrapped it in the silk cloth it had been presented in and gave it to her.

"I am my mother's daughter," I said as I did. "But I am very different from her. I wasn't when you first met me, at Framlingham Castle. But I have learned things since then, things that she never did."

"I remember how you didn't want to wear the livery of the queen," she said. "But you learned to do so. And now you choose your garments for yourself."

I stood up. "Put the tiara away. I have finery enough for tomorrow."

HISTORICAL NOTE

Lady Margaret's marriage produced four sons, two of whom survived to adulthood and fathered families of their own. Her descendants continue to the present. She died in 1596, having outlived all seven women who had once stood ahead of her in the succession, except Queen Elizabeth, who had followed her childless sister Mary as queen. After Elizabeth, the throne passed to the descendants of Mary Queen of Scots, the succession as set by King Henry VIII and King Edward VI no longer being relevant.

A NOTE TO THE READER

Dear Reader,

Thank you for reading *The Queen's Rival*, the first in my new series of novels about the ebb and flow of the Tudor succession in the sixteenth and early seventeenth centuries. Are there any new stories to tell about the Tudors? I have found some that are either not well known or about which I have ideas that differ from what has been generally accepted. Although they are works of fiction, all adhere to the known facts about the people and events presented. As a novelist, I fill in the spaces between those often scant facts with motives and actions they suggest to my imagination, and which seem to me might very well be true. For example, there is no proof of the possible murders Margaret learns of in her family's history, but their pattern, when viewed as a forest and not individual trees, seems otherwise to me, especially when the surrounding ambitions are considered. I also, for motives and behaviour, try to stay consistent with the time period and especially the unusual social status of the characters, whose experiences would certainly have rendered them different not only from modern people, but even those of their own times. It was inevitable that those born to power would have been taught almost from birth to fight to hold what was theirs, with ambition becoming a primary motivator in later life. Often those ambitions, especially for women, played out through their children, and it is those stories which are the basis for this series.

Although I had long had a passing interest in the Tudors, it came more into focus after completion of my first novel *Booth's*

Daughter, and I wanted to move beyond the theatre history which had occupied my career. Fortunately, the emergence of the Internet at around the same time made enormous amounts of previously obscure and difficult-to-access historical material available, including the Tudors; not only about the people involved but the places where their individual stories played out. And with that, I gradually became confident enough as a twenty-first-century American man to write a story about a sixteenth-century British woman: Margaret Clifford.

Once again, thank you for reading the novel. If you liked it, I would be grateful if you would post a review on **Amazon** and **Goodreads**. And please keep an eye out for the other novels which are coming!

Thank you!

Raymond Wemmlinger

Sapere Books is an exciting new publisher of brilliant fiction and popular history.

To find out more about our latest releases and our monthly bargain books visit our website: **saperebooks.com**

Printed in Great Britain
by Amazon